"Rappelling," I answered, like climbers are supposed to do. With that, keeping the rope taut, I backed toward the edge.

A look over my shoulder and I saw the surf break right on the seal. Another wave that big and the animal would be out to sea and drowning.

Leaning way back, I started feeding rope through the figure eight and went over the edge with small steps. I got a little sideways but adjusted with my legs and kept my balance.

My feet hit the beach. I got off the rope and quickly looked around for the seal. The surf surged around my knees and rocked me, but I stayed upright. I thought I'd lost the seal for sure when I saw it being carried past me. I reached out and grabbed it.

"How is it?" Neal called down.

"Pretty bad. Wounds are infected."

"Jackie can give it antibiotics."

"Hear that?" I said to the seal. "No worries. We're going to fix you up."

BOOKS BY WILL HOBBS

Changes in Latitudes

Bearstone

Downriver

The Big Wander

Beardance

Kokopelli's Flute

Far North

Ghost Canoe

Beardream

River Thunder

Howling Hill

The Maze

Jason's Gold

Down the Yukon

Wild Man Island

Leaving Protection

JACKIE'S WILD SEATTLE

Will Hobbs

HarperTrophy®
An Imprint of HarperCollins*Publishers*

to Kaye Baxter, Bob Jones,
and Jeff Eagle Walker Guidry

Jackie's Wild Seattle
Copyright © 2003 by Will Hobbs

Library of Congress Cataloging-in-Publication Data
Hobbs, Will.
    Jackie's wild Seattle / Will Hobbs.
        p.   cm.
    Summary: Fourteen-year-old Shannon and her little brother,
Cody, spend the summer with their uncle, helping at a wildlife
rescue center named Jackie's Wild Seattle.
    ISBN 0-688-17474-4 — ISBN 0-06-051631-3 (lib. bdg.)
    ISBN 0-380-73311-0 (pbk.)
    [1. Uncles—Fiction. 2. Brothers and sisters—Fiction.
3. Wildlife rescue—Fiction. 4. Seattle (Wash.)—Fiction.]
I. Title.
PZ7.H6524 Jad 2003   2002013386
[Fic]—dc21   CIP
                                                  AC

Typography by Amy Ryan

First Harper Trophy edition, 2004
Visit us on the World Wide Web!
www.harperchildrens.com

1

SORRY ABOUT
THE DOG HAIR

I didn't even recognize him when he headed toward us at the crowded baggage carousel. Just some confused guy with a shaved head, that's what I thought at first, but then he called my name.

I did a double take. Could this be our Uncle Neal?

"Shannie, over here," he called as he came closer.

I recognized his voice, but otherwise I was drawing a blank. I was expecting him to look like his snapshot on our refrigerator back home, with curly black hair, a full face, and a neatly trimmed beard. This Neal had a thin face and was clean-shaven from skull to chin.

The uncle I was expecting had the strong, chiseled arms and legs of a climber. This version was almost skinny and had no muscle definition. Plus he had a tattoo—the word *Sage* on his left arm. My mother had never said anything about her brother having a tattoo.

All the same, it had to be him. I could see my mother in

the lines around his steel gray eyes, the shape of his lips, and the dimple on his chin.

"I go by Shannon now," I muttered as he gave me a hug. Only Cody could get away with calling me Shannie these days.

Neal tried to shake with Cody, but my little brother shrank back. "He isn't shy," I said, "he just hates shaking hands."

"No I don't," Cody protested. "It's just weird, that's all."

I looked from Cody to this stranger-uncle and back, feeling so not okay about the next nine weeks. Out of nervousness I checked my watch. During the flight I'd turned it back three hours. Here in Seattle, it was only nine-thirty in the morning. We'd started our trip at La Guardia airport in New York, checking in at 5 A.M. I couldn't help yawning.

"Longest day of the year," Neal said. "June twenty-first. Say, I got a call from your folks. They said to tell you their plane took off on time, ninety minutes after yours. They've sure got a long way to go, halfway around the world."

Cody bit his lip. Me, I didn't say anything. We didn't really know our uncle very well. Basically we talked to him on the phone every Christmas. This whole summer was going to be quite a stretch.

Uncle Neal changed the subject. "Cody, you'll never guess what I'm doing these days. You'll be surprised. I'm driving an ambulance."

Cody looked skeptical.

"Really. Wait till you see it."

We pulled luggage from the carousel as Uncle Neal established our ages, fourteen and seven. I was still stunned by his makeover, especially the shaved head. It was a popular look, but definitely not my favorite.

Up close, Neal had a gamey smell, which wasn't exactly

appealing. His T-shirt and jeans were covered with dog hair. His eyes were bloodshot, and there were dirt smudges on his clothes. He looked tired. Underneath his cheerfulness, he looked worried, maybe even grim. My mother said he was thirty-nine, but he came off older. "What's with the new look?" I asked, deciding to go for it.

My uncle ran his hand over his skull. "You mean this? No muss, no fuss. What do you think, Cody? Should I get an earring like the NBA players?"

"Maybe not," Cody said. "Who's Sage?"

"My partner. You'll meet her shortly."

"Girlfriend?" I asked.

"Sort of."

"Have you gone back to work at Boeing?"

"Nope, still haven't."

My biggest hope for the summer was that we could do some rock climbing together. Here was a guy who'd climbed Mount Rainier in a whiteout and helped rescue the survivors of a group that had its tents blown off the mountain near the summit. "Are you still climbing? Still doing search and rescue?" I asked casually, keeping my enthusiasm in check.

"Naw," Neal said. "I don't really do that stuff anymore."

Cody and I waited at the curb with our mound of luggage, which was mostly mine. Nine weeks away called for two-thirds of everything I owned. We waited for what felt like a long time. Everything was confusing, edgy, and noisy. The lanes closest to the curb were clogged with cars stopping to pick up arriving passengers. Just like back at La Guardia, security guards and soldiers on the lookout for terrorists were adding to the tension.

My eyes were drawn to a large maroon van in the outer

lane. JACKIE'S WILD SEATTLE was written in large letters across
the side, with WILDLIFE RESCUE AND REHAB underneath, plus
an 800 number. At either end of the lettering was a seal's
face, all eyes and whiskers, and the white head of a bald eagle.
"Hey, that's Uncle Neal driving," Cody yelled. "That must be
the ambulance! Look, Shan, check out his passenger!"

A very alert black-and-white dog was riding shotgun. Neal
managed to thread his way to the curb in front of us, where
he lurched to a stop and jumped out. "Is that your partner,
by any chance?" Cody asked as all three of us grabbed luggage. "Is that Sage?"

"You're quick, Cody. Yes indeed, that person up front
wearing the furry suit is my partner. And this van is an
extension of my body. I've already put forty-five thousand
miles on it this year."

Neal lifted up the back, and I found out where the gamey
smell on his clothes was coming from. The van reeked of it.
There were feathers all over, a few old duffel bags, metal
boxes, fiberglass kennel carriers of various sizes, a giant
fishing net. "Is there going to be enough room for our
stuff?" I wondered aloud.

"Has to be," Neal said, pulling some of the kennel carriers out onto the pavement. "It'll just take some rearrang-
ing." He was huffing and puffing, and his forehead was
beaded with sweat.

"Let me do that," I said. I was surprised how out of shape
he was.

"You're dressed too nice," Neal protested.

"Just jeans and a top."

"I mean, you're too clean."

Obviously, teenage girls weren't the sort of wildlife Neal
was familiar with. He was going to treat me like I was frag-

ile when I was anything but. "No problem," I said, grabbing a kennel carrier in each hand. "I'm adaptable. So is Cody. Aren't you, Cody?"

"Not too small and not too big," Cody said. Neal and I looked at each other. Then it dawned on both of us that my little brother was talking about the dog.

"Border collie," Neal told him.

I said to Neal, "You organize things inside, I'll hand this stuff to you."

He took my suggestion. His eyes met mine, and he said, "Thanks for being adaptable, Shannon. That's really going to help."

"Mom said you live at the beach these days?"

"I did the last couple years, until today."

"Hey, Shannie," Cody called, "this one has something in it." He was on his knees looking into one of the carriers on the pavement.

Suddenly two security guards followed by a soldier came running right at us. "What's in there?" shouted the one in the lead. He was very young, with an unconvincing mustache. His nameplate said DUFFY. One hand was at his hip, on his gun.

Cody took in the three stressed-out men in uniform towering over him. In a very small voice, my brother answered, "Four baby raccoons."

Neal bent to lift the carrier so they could see inside its door.

"Don't!" ordered Duffy. With a swift motion, he signaled his partner, Wattle, to get down and take a look. The soldier, meanwhile, unslung his rifle and stepped back to cover them. With a glance I saw a crowd of people stopped in their tracks, mostly alarmed but with a few smiles sprinkled in. Did we look like terrorists?

On his hands and knees, Wattle peeked cautiously through the carrier door. "Raccoons," he reported.

"You're good to go," Duffy growled. "Next time, don't linger."

"Thank you," Neal said. "We appreciate your vigilance."

The three backed off. As if somebody had thrown a switch, all the onlookers were back in motion.

Uncle Neal slammed the back hatch shut and grabbed the carrier with the raccoons, then went to the side door and threw it open. "Let's get out of here. Backseat, Sage." His dog obeyed immediately. "Jump in, Cody. I'll put these baby raccoons between you and Sage so you can keep your eye on these rascals."

Cody hesitated. "Actually, I'd rather sit right next to Sage."

"Nice idea, but she doesn't like kids. Nothing personal."

I took the passenger seat up front. "Sorry about all the dog hair," Neal said as he slid behind the wheel. He grabbed the Mariners cap from the dash, slapped it on his shiny head, and jammed the key into the ignition. The van started with a roar, and we took off.

2

CHANGE IS INEVITABLE

In between me and Neal, spilling down to the floor of the van, was enough junk to fill a chest of drawers, including a clipboard, various scraps of notes and ballpoint pens, a pager, a cell phone, and a Starbucks cup. I checked over my shoulder to make sure Cody had buckled up. He had.

"Who's Jackie?" Cody asked while looking wistfully at the dog on the other side of the carrier. Sage avoided his gaze. Cody had always wanted a dog, but we lived in a house with too small a yard on too busy a street.

"Jackie's the head of a three-ring circus," Neal replied.

Cody rummaged in his backpack and pulled out his Game Boy. The border collie looked nervous as the electronic beeps and music from the little machine began. I wondered if Neal was going to ask Cody to turn it off. He didn't. If Neal had, Cody might have had to pull out his chewed-up security blankie. He'd already had one setback, the dog not being friendly, and I could tell he was feeling more than a little sorry for himself.

We drove north on the freeway. It was a dazzling blue-sky day in Seattle. You could see clear past the skyscrapers—not many compared to Manhattan—to the Space Needle. I pointed in its direction.

Cody spotted it and snapped out of his funk. "The Space Needle is the *whole reason* I wanted to come to Seattle," he told his uncle dramatically. "Hey, Shan, you should see these baby raccoons. They woke up and they're all over each other."

Neal swung by his old place in West Seattle, the apartment he'd just left. It was right across the street from the beach. "I just have to pick up my mail," he said. "And say good-bye to Charlie."

"Who's Charlie?" Cody asked as we got out. He was looking all around, and so was I.

"Retired columnist for the *Seattle Times*. Lives downstairs."

Just across the street, people were jogging, flying kites, throwing Frisbees, tanning, playing volleyball. I said, "Are you sure this isn't southern California?"

Neal checked his mailbox and visited with the old man who lived in the lower unit while we ran up the outside stairway and into Neal's old apartment. Cody sailed right through it onto the deck overlooking the beach, and I followed. "Let's stay here," Cody said. "We can play on the beach all summer."

"Uncle Neal already moved out," I reminded him.

Cody's face went tragic. I said, "Whatever look you were going for just now, you missed." Actually, I was pretty disappointed myself. Here was the chance for me to wear my new two-piece. This summer I could finally do justice to a bathing suit.

I turned back into the apartment and quickly discovered it was strictly a studio—no bedrooms, no privacy.

I walked back out onto the deck and joined Cody at the railing. He was still enraptured with the beach. "This place would be so perfect, Shannie!"

"We're talking shoe box," I said. "Take a better look inside."

His eyes started to get misty. "We could sleep out on the deck, don't you see? This is the whole reason I came!"

I cracked up. "No it isn't, Cody. You had no idea about this place. You came because Mom and Dad are going to Pakistan, don't you remember?"

Neal, I realized, was standing right behind us, getting another look at his overdramatic nephew. "It was brave of you guys to come," he said, "even if there wasn't really much choice. We'll make the most of it, believe me. And hey, change is inevitable, except from vending machines."

"I think I saw that once on a bumper sticker," I said.

To which Neal replied, "Without bumper stickers, wisdom itself would be impossible."

"Is that from a bumper sticker, too?"

"Not as far as I know. I just made it up."

I was impressed. "For the record, Uncle Neal, it wasn't really fair for Mom and Dad to spring this on you—and us—with only three weeks' notice."

Cody piled on. "I have a lot of friends back home. Shannon does too. I'm on a soccer team. Shan was going to go to her camp in the Adirondacks to go rock climbing and stuff."

Neal stroked the short beard that was missing from his chin. I thought he might show some interest in how much climbing I'd done—two straight weeks, two summers in a row—but he didn't. Instead he said, "It was a surprise for all of us."

"Yeah," Cody said with a frown. "That man from Doctors Without Borders called and said they needed Mom *and* Dad."

"At first Dad was going to go alone," I explained, "and then when he got back, Mom would go. That was the original plan."

Before we left home I'd hardly let myself picture what this would be like, having both of them so far away for so long and in such a risky part of the world. I'd be holding my breath the whole summer. I think I was half expecting them to change their minds and not go through with it.

My brother looked up to me and said, "We're proud of them, aren't we, Shannie?"

"We sure are," I said, which of course I was. "Mom did say we could veto it," I added to Neal. "Cody and I talked it over a lot. It was obvious how bad they wanted to go, both of them together. We gave them the green light."

Cody said to Neal, "It's not as dangerous over there as people think, isn't that right?"

Uncle Neal didn't look so sure about that. But he nodded and said reassuringly, "They'll be okay in western Pakistan, Cody, especially in a big refugee camp."

"Except there's lots of people with only one leg, because of all the land mines."

Before this got out of hand—Cody was very big on disasters—I said, "The land mines aren't in the refugee camps, Cody. They're over in Afghanistan. That's where the refugees came from."

"I know, Mom told me all about it."

Neal jumped in with, "Say, are you guys hungry?"

"Are you kidding?" Cody shouted. "Do you have a Taco Bell? I could get a seven-layer burrito!"

"No, but there's a great deli just down the street."

All of a sudden, Cody went miserable. "What if they don't have anything I like? I'm a very picky eater. It's not my fault. I can't help it."

"It's just something he has to live with," I couldn't resist adding.

"I was just teasing you," Neal said to Cody. "Your mother told me about your 'dietary restrictions.' She said you eat only hot dogs or corn dogs, peanut-butter-and-jelly sandwiches on white bread, mac and cheese, pepperoni pizza, soft flour tortillas with refried beans and grated cheddar cheese slightly melted, certain kinds of cold cereal with whole milk, certain fruits, certain kinds of ice cream. . . ."

"Pinch me," I said. "She told you all that? Has she lost her mind?"

Cody piped up with, "She forgot cookies and candy bars. There aren't many of those I don't like, Uncle Neal. Oreos are my favorite."

I couldn't believe it. My mother had finally caved in, declared surrender, and run up the white flag on nutrition and a balanced diet. All I could figure was, she was afraid he'd have a meltdown on her brother.

"So let's run for the border," Neal said.

"Taco Bell!" Cody shouted with three quick fist pumps. "Things are looking up in Codyland!"

Neal said good-bye to the old man, the retired columnist downstairs, and we were on our way to find Cody a burrito. Staring at the border collie who didn't like kids, Cody said sadly, "I guess it's okay about not living at the beach. I wouldn't want to live upstairs from a retired communist anyway."

3

THE VIEW
FROM THE NEEDLE

All the way to the Taco Bell, Uncle Neal's pager was beeping, collecting phone numbers for him to call back. He took the pager, the cell phone, and his clipboard inside and returned his calls while he was eating. The clipboard was for jotting down directions. After we'd eaten, there was just enough time to talk. I got a few things figured out about my mysterious uncle:

1) Neal's beach apartment was too cramped for him to keep the weights and exercise equipment I remembered from our visit to Seattle before Cody was born.

2) These days he was too busy for all that. Driving the ambulance for Jackie's Wild Seattle was a 24/7 job.

3) Uncle Neal didn't get paid. He was a volunteer.

4) Boeing was starting to build more airplanes again, but so far they hadn't called him back to work.

5) Uncle Neal wasn't broke. He could afford us for nine weeks.

6) Neal wasn't sure he was going to go back to being an aeronautical engineer.

7) We were all going to live at Jackie's house, at the wildlife center, which was an hour northeast of Seattle, way out in the woods.

That last item we learned on our way out to the parking lot. Cody immediately liked the sound of living in the woods, but I wasn't so sure. I said cautiously, "I suppose being at the wildlife center wouldn't be boring."

With a grin, Neal said, "Not a chance. And Jackie has all kinds of room."

"Does she live alone?"

"No, she has two golden retrievers. Who like kids, by the way."

"Forget the retrievers," I said. "What's Jackie like?"

"Ferociously difficult to get along with."

Even Cody could see Neal was kidding. I asked how old Jackie was.

"Older than dirt, according to her, but don't believe it. She started the center after her kids had flown the nest."

I had to get to the bottom of this. "You're moving up there on account of us? Is that the reason?"

"Partly, but it'll be better for me too. The wildlife center is my life these days. Makes more sense for me to base out of Jackie's instead of dropping animals off there, then driving an hour home for a few winks. I'll burn quite a bit less gas, and gas is one of Jackie's biggest expenses. Do me a favor and e-mail your mother about our change of address, will you?"

We were rolling again. "So how come you didn't tell Mom you were just about to move?"

"I didn't want to upset her apple cart. In order for her to

leave on short notice, I figured she needed things to be simple, not complicated."

"Okay," I said. "I can understand that."

"I think the world of your mother, Shannon."

"She does of you, too. The part I can't quite figure is how come you two aren't closer? You hardly ever see each other."

Neal just shook his head. "Don't have a good answer for that one. Three thousand miles and poor excuses. Modern life, I guess."

With a look over my shoulder I could tell that Cody hadn't been listening to a word from up front. He was peeking through the door of the carrier, all absorbed with the baby raccoons.

"So I threw you a curve, Shannon, about us living out in the country," Neal continued. "It isn't what you expected. I'm sorry about that."

"I haven't even seen the place yet, so there's nothing to be sorry about. It'll probably be fine. I've always liked the outdoors, nature and all that, but more as a getaway, like the Adirondacks for climbing camp, that kind of stuff. I'm pretty used to living a stone's throw from the city. I like it— I like all the go-go-go. But don't worry, I like new things too."

Our conversation trailed off. I was left wondering how much Neal's taking us for the summer was out of duty, and how much was because he wanted to get to know us better.

I turned the same question around and asked it of myself. Mostly I was doing this for my mom, just like Neal was doing it for his sister. Now what, with nine weeks stretching over the horizon like an eternity?

These last few weeks I'd been up and down and all over

the place about the idea of spending the summer with my uncle. "The kindest person you'll ever meet," my mother had said, but among my friends who was famous for looking at the world through rose-colored glasses. Yes, I was looking forward to the time with him, but he better be worth it. This was my entire summer we were talking about.

One thing I'd already figured out about getting closer to Uncle Neal. There were going to be some hazards—for instance, him smelling like a raccoon.

Just ahead, Seattle's skyscrapers were looming. Out of the blue, my little brother announced that Seattle was the third-riskiest city for earthquakes in the whole United States.

"Don't I know," Uncle Neal agreed.

"Wait a minute!" Cody practically shouted. "You were here for the 6.8!"

"I certainly was. You should have seen my apartment. Every single thing on the walls came down, and most of my dishes and glassware walked right out of the cabinets and crashed on the floor. It was quite a mess. Fortunately, nobody got killed in that quake."

"I know, there's a picture in my *Book of Disasters*."

"His favorite book," I explained.

"I'll show it to you later, Uncle Neal. The picture is of a place in Seattle called Pioneer Square. The bricks fell off the buildings."

"I could take you there right now," Neal told him, "but I have to warn you, they've picked up all the bricks and stuck them back on the buildings. Or would you rather go to the top of the Space Needle?"

It wasn't much of a contest. We left Sage and the raccoons in the shade of a parking garage and took the mono-

rail to the Seattle Center, where the Space Needle was the
featured attraction. A quick ride on an express elevator, and
we were high above the city.

Forget about the stunning views of the downtown skyline,
the neighborhoods and Lake Washington, the harbor and
the cruise ships, and the island-sprinkled waterways of
Puget Sound leading out to the Pacific. Cody had eyes only
for the gigantic glacier-covered mountain to the southeast.
"Mount Rainier," he whispered reverently. "That mountain is
one of the biggest disasters waiting to happen in the whole
world. When it blows its top, it's going to be *major*."

"I hate to disappoint you," his uncle said, "but that might
be thousands of years from now."

"Or this summer, while we're here," Cody insisted.

"I can't tell if you really want to see that or really don't
want to see that."

"Both," I answered for Cody. "Enough already about disasters, before we move on to tidal waves."

Uncle Neal gave Cody some quarters for the telescope, so
he could look at Mount Doom to his heart's content. We sat
at a nearby table and talked. Neal said right away, "Tell me
about Cody's disaster fixation."

"Obsession, you might call it."

"How far back does it go?"

"A little more than nine months. September 11, 2001, to
be exact."

"Oh well, that explains a lot."

I lowered my voice and told him all about it, how my parents had gone off to work, I was headed to school, and Cody
was at our neighbor's across the street—Joey's mom drives
them to school. "They were just getting into the car when all
these people came running down the street, toward the

riverbank. You remember where we live, don't you, half a block from the Hudson River?"

"I sure do. You're two minutes' walk from that amazing view of Manhattan."

"That's right. So there's Cody, suddenly hearing everyone shouting that one of the twin towers at the World Trade Center had been hit by an airplane. An accident, everybody thought. Mrs. Donnelly and the boys ran down to the end of the block to see. The building was already sending up that huge column of smoke. They got there about five minutes before the hijackers flew the second airliner into the second tower."

"So Cody actually saw that happen."

"He sure did. He saw the airplane coming, saw it hit the building, saw the ball of flame and everything. Everybody knew that the twin towers were gigantic office buildings with tens of thousands of people working inside. Mrs. Donnelly said everybody just stood there on the bluff, petrified. There was nothing to do but watch the tallest skyscrapers in New York City burn. Suddenly, from the top down, one of them just collapsed. They saw it fall, saw the dust clouds boil up and blot out lower Manhattan. Joey's mom said that people started crying, screaming. Cody and Joey were really, really scared."

Uncle Neal, biting his lip, was at a loss for words. I finished up quickly. It was still so hard to talk about. "The three of them ran back to Joey's house and they saw the second tower come down on TV. Cody has a best friend, Mike Wyatt, whose dad worked on the ninety-fifth floor of one of the towers. Cody had even been in his office once."

"I take it Mike's father lost his life."

"Yes. And Cody's having a real hard time getting over it."

Neal winced and said, "Everyone in the country's still trying to adjust, but the closer you were and the more involved, the worse it would affect you. Cody saw it with his own eyes, and he hadn't even turned seven."

I dabbed my eyes with my fingers. "Sorry," I said.

"Don't be, Shannon. I understand."

"I guess I haven't gotten over it myself. I have nightmares too, not that I ever told my parents about them. They had enough on their plate with Cody. He took it so hard. Cody knew Mike's dad so well—he was their soccer coach. Our family went to his funeral. There was no body or anything. Most of those three thousand people who died were just ground to dust."

"Cody will come through it," Neal said softly.

"Mom says he'll be okay," I said. "He hasn't had a nightmare in a couple months, at least that she knows about, which is partly how she talked herself into thinking it was okay to go to Pakistan with Dad."

"Is there another part?"

"Well, she thought going to Seattle might help get Cody's mind off it. Everything would be so far away and so different. She says to just let him work it through. I guess she ought to know, being a pediatrician and all."

"So his disaster obsession may not be such a bad thing."

"That's what Mom thinks. She says it's part of his healing process. Eventually he should move on to something else. You should see his library of disaster books, all natural disasters, by the way. It would be kind of refreshing to see him go back to *Captain Underpants*."

Cody was off the telescope and soon we were back in the van and rolling again. Neal had new messages and calls to make. Some could wait, but there was one he had to attend to right away. Somebody's dog had torn up a possum in Redmond, Washington, famous for Bill Gates and his Microsoft Corporation.

Before Neal even started the van he put a sturdy yellow vest on his border collie. It was heavy canvas with a cloth liner, and covered the dog's back, sides, and shoulders. The vest fastened at her neck and around her middle with plastic buckles that Neal cinched tight. "What in the world is it?" Cody asked.

"Flak jacket," Neal replied, suddenly intense. "Sage wears it for a hot rescue, which involves finding the animal."

"So what's a cold rescue?"

"That's when somebody hands you a baby bunny or an injured sparrow in a cardboard box. Sage and I, we live for the hot rescues."

"Sage looks tense," Cody observed as we sped away.

"Just terribly, terribly alert," Neal said. "*Longjaw*, Sage, *Longjaw*."

Suddenly his dog was as focused as a ballistic missile. "What was that?" I asked.

"I just told her what animal we were after. I only use that word when we're in the hunt mode. You two, don't ever, ever say that word to her. It's only for business, and I'm the only one who says it. I can't just use the word *possum*. Then every time somebody said 'possum,' she'd think she was supposed to go find one. So we have our own code."

The highway took us over a floating bridge across the long lake behind the city, Lake Washington. Ten minutes later Neal pointed out a bumper sticker and joked that we must be getting close to Redmond. It said WE ARE MICROSOFT. RESISTANCE IS FUTILE. YOU WILL BE ASSIMILATED.

Neal found the neighborhood he was looking for, and the

house. It wasn't Bill Gates's mansion but it was about four times the size of our house on Liberty Place back in Weehawken. An elegant lady met us at the door. "Maybe I could have caught it, but I was afraid. I called all over the place. Finally I called the police and they said they'd call you."

"I'm glad you were persistent," Neal said as he pulled on a heavy pair of gloves.

"I'm sure it's hopeless. It crawled off and is probably long gone."

"No, the possum's still here."

The woman looked at him strangely. "How do you know?"

"My dog told me as soon as we got out of the van."

Cody and I looked at each other. Somehow we had missed this.

The backyard was enormous. Two acres, the lady said. It was basically a jungle of trees, bushes, and blackberry vines. *Hopeless* is the word I would have used too. Sage whined impatiently at Neal's side. Neal picked up the kennel carrier and said something I couldn't quite hear. Sage took off like a shot.

About ten seconds later, in a far corner of the yard, the border collie came to a screeching halt in front of a thicket of rhododendrons. When Neal caught up, she led him inside. Sage's partner came back out a minute later with the bizarre-looking beastie, all jaws and teeth, in the carrier.

Cody was, for once, speechless.

4

THE END
OF THE BEGINNING

Back on the freeway, we headed south into Bellevue and stopped at a veterinary clinic to pick up a crow, a pigeon, two squirrels, and a cottontail rabbit. Most were victims of house cats. Neal said there were eleven different vets in the Seattle area who helped Jackie, for free. Sometimes it was just a matter of holding the animals until Neal could come and get them. Other times it involved care, including operations. Sometimes the vets came to Jackie's to do the operations.

We were crossing back over Lake Washington, this time on I-90. Just as we came out of the Mercer Island tunnel and onto the bridge, Neal said over his shoulder, "It's pretty quiet in the back. How's everything in Codyland?"

"Actually, I'm having a little problem."

Cody's guilty voice hinted at a *major* problem. I looked over my shoulder so fast I could've gotten whiplash. There were the baby raccoons, on his lap and on the move and all over the place. "Cody," I shrieked. "How in the world did they get out?"

"It was an accident. The latch was really hard. I was just trying to figure out how it works."

In a heartbeat, all four baby raccoons were on Uncle Neal—one on each shoulder, one on the back of his neck, one on top of his Mariners cap. I would have laughed, but he was doing seventy and we were in heavy traffic, right in the middle of the bridge.

One of the raccoons suddenly pulled off Neal's sunglasses. The people in the car beside us thought this was amusing. They whipped out a video camera and started filming. It was so *not* amusing. Neal had the steering wheel in a death grip and was battling to stay in control.

Neal told me to pull the raccoons off him and put them in the backseat. But as soon as I'd drop one on the floor behind me, it scrambled to the front. It was hopeless; one was on his head again with its tail in his face. "Sorry," Cody whimpered. We were off the bridge but heading into another tunnel.

The first exit after the tunnel, Neal bailed off the interstate. "Good thing raccoons are friendly and mellow," Cody said solemnly as we lurched to a stop.

"They're anything but," Neal said. He was shaken, but trying his best to stay calm. "Fortunately these are babies."

"How come Sage doesn't like kids?" Cody asked.

I gave him The Look. "Changing the subject, are you, Cody?"

"It was just a human mistake, Shannie. I'll never do it again." He started to sniffle.

"Of course you won't," Neal said, wiping the sweat from his forehead. Just then his cell phone rang. Neal put his fingers to his lips. Cody got the hint and quit sniffling.

Uncle Neal listened intently. This was some kind of big deal. "Fledgling bald eagle fell out of the nest in Discovery Park!" he exclaimed as he hung up. "Everybody, grab the nearest raccoon."

Neal and I each caught one, and Cody caught two. Sage seemed to be trying to look the other way, like she couldn't bear watching a bunch of amateurs. Cody managed to stuff all the babies back into the carrier and close the door. "Good job!" Uncle Neal shouted. "We're on our way to Discovery Park for an eagle!"

Our driver was off to the races. An eagle, obviously, didn't come along every day.

Uncle Neal pulled into a neighborhood below the park and above the ship canal that connects Lake Washington to Puget Sound. He lurched to a stop practically in the middle of the street, switched on the lights that flashed yellow on the top of the van, and leaped into action. We tore through a backyard and up the hillside toward the park.

Huffing and puffing, Neal explained that finding the nest was going to be easy. It was one of the very few bald eagle nests in Seattle, and he'd been there before. "I just hope dogs haven't gotten to the bird," he wheezed. He had to set the carrier down and rest. Neal let me take it. Weird, I thought. He must have been doing this sort of stuff every day, yet he was totally out of shape. Did he spend his free time on the couch watching TV?

When we got close, the spot was obvious. Underneath a cluster of tall spruce trees, people were standing around keeping watch. They cheered when they saw Neal on the run and the carrier in my hand. I spotted the nest, a huge tangle of sticks high in one of the trees.

The crowd parted for Neal and he went to his knees close to the bird. The eagle fledgling was way bigger than I would have guessed; it looked practically full grown. It hissed at Neal and flopped around something awful. The feathers on its head and tail weren't white like a bald eagle's. That must take time, I thought. Somebody said that a car had back-fired three or four times in the street below just before it fell. "Its wings might be broken," somebody said.

"Likely so," Neal agreed.

Neal was wearing a heavy pair of gloves. With a move that was nearly too quick to see, he had the eagle contained and tucked against his side.

People cheered. "Thank you, everybody," Neal said. His eyes were moist, which was as touching to see as the hurt eagle. "We'll do everything we can, I guarantee you that. Cody, would you open that carrier for me?"

Neal gently placed the bird inside. Cody alertly swung the door shut. Neal said, "Let's get the ambulance on the road, guys." He turned to the people and handed out some sort of small cards. They were donation cards for Jackie's Wild Seattle. "Thanks, everybody," he said softly, and we were gone.

Back at the van, the baby raccoons were fussing and crying. "Hungry, real hungry," Neal explained as he punched up Jackie's number. "I just hope Jackie's there. She's crazy about any kind of raptor, but eagles are her heart's delight—eagles and red-tailed hawks."

She was there. "Call one of your bird vets," Neal told her first thing. He was beside himself with excitement. "Fledgling bald eagle inbound from Discovery Park. Took a bad fall, both wings possibly fractured."

A pause and then, "What do you mean is that all? Have

you lost your mind, Jackie?"

We heard squawking on the other end. Neal made a show of holding the phone away from his ear. Then he said, "Oh yeah, got them, too. They appear to be in the pink of health. Two *Homo sapiens* from New Jersey. Siblings that migrated west for the summer. The male appears to be seven years old and the young woman fourteen. Cody and Shannon Young, if you please, coming your way in an hour's time along with four raccoon babies, a possum, assorted birds, two squirrels, and a bunny. These baby raccoons are *real* hungry. Got a call on my way to the airport. The people live-trapped and relocated the mother without realizing she had babies under their house—until they started crying their little lungs out, that is. Familiar story. Start mixing formula or go milk your goat, Jackie, whatever it is you do."

Neal hung up. Was our uncle ever pumped. "Man oh man, how I love this job, but did Jackie ever get on my case."

"What for?" we both asked at once.

"For not bringing you hours ago, like I talked about. I should've called her when I picked you up. I got so excited seeing you guys, it slipped my mind. Supper's ready as soon as we hand off the eagle. No doubt one of her raptor vets is already on the road."

What a day it had been, and still the sun wasn't even close to setting as we reached the little town of Cedar Glen and drove out a country road lined with tall cedar trees. I noticed a red warning light appear on the dash, then a second one. Neal had noticed them too, but didn't look worried.

For once the kid in the backseat had nothing to say. The last hour had been real quiet, each of us deep in our own thoughts. Talk about a long day. I thought about my parents,

how far along they might be on their journey while we were
so close to the end of ours, or at least the end of the beginning.

I guessed my parents were only as far as France. They
had a long layover in Paris before they caught a plane to
Karachi, Pakistan. Then they'd have to catch another flight
to Islamabad. Somebody from Doctors Without Borders
would meet them there and drive them to the refugee camp
in the desert outside Peshawar, close to the Afghanistan
border.

I was worried about how we'd stay in touch. E-mail was
our best bet if there was a telephone in or near the refugee
camp. My parents had a handheld device that they could
press to the mouthpiece of a telephone. Theoretically they
could send and receive e-mails that way. But we weren't
supposed to count on it.

My eye caught the small JACKIE'S WILD SEATTLE sign set
back from the road. We turned in to the driveway. I breathed
in the aromatic cedars. I thought about those deserts in
Afghanistan and all those refugees. Pictures I'd seen came
to mind of people cutting down their last trees for firewood,
slaughtering their last animals, abandoning their homes and
walking hundreds of miles to the feeding camps across the
border. I thought about the disasters they'd suffered,
drought, starvation, disease, and wars that had been going
on for more than twenty years. I was so fiercely proud of my
parents going to help, my eyes were brimming.

As we drove up Jackie's long gravel driveway I was
almost ashamed for our green, well-watered land and all our
blessings. I blinked away my tears and saw a small mob of
people waiting for us in the parking area in front of the
wildlife center, a cluster of nondescript one-story buildings.

The old two-story Victorian house on the right, a "fixer-upper" you might call it, had to be Jackie's home. A gray-haired woman stepped forward from the group with two golden retrievers at her side. She walked with a limp, and somehow I knew this was Jackie. Cody and I got out of the van and followed shyly behind Neal, who was holding the eagle carrier high, like he was the Statue of Liberty and the bird was his torch.

A younger woman with red hair came to Jackie's side and took the carrier. Jackie called Cody and me by name and took us under her wings. "I bet you're hungry," she said.

From the corner of my eye I caught sight of someone standing apart from all the rest, sort of behind one of the cars, just watching. He was my age or a little older with wild-looking black hair and intense dark eyes. He seemed to want to join in, but wouldn't. He was holding himself apart, and I was wondering why.

Jackie introduced us to her evening-shift volunteers, then pointed out the young red-haired woman heading into the clinic with the eagle as Rosie. Jackie didn't identify the boy on the fringe, and I wondered what that was all about. Curious, I glanced back at him and took in his off-balance stance, hands shoved deep into the pockets of his jeans, head cocked at a proud, skeptical angle, eyes that in the brief second he looked my way were appealing for help or hope or I couldn't tell what, maybe understanding.

A lost soul, that's how he struck me, sending out a beacon before he went down, but that was only a fleeting impression. Moments later he melted around the back of the cars and started walking down the driveway without looking back.

The jet lag had my eyelids at half mast. It may have been

early evening in western Washington, but Cody and I were still on Weehawken time. Cody actually fell asleep over his lasagna. He never really woke up as we trooped him upstairs. Jackie had three separate rooms for us up there, with thoughtful touches in each, like scented lotion and a vase of fresh-cut flowers on my nightstand.

Checking in on Cody, I discovered he'd crash-landed face-down onto his bed. I took off his shoes, then let sleeping dogs lie. Myself, all that I unpacked was a sleep shirt. I thought a prayer for my parents, wherever they were, slid between sweet, clothesline-fresh sheets, mused momentarily about how strange it was that Jackie and this farmhouse, as she called it, had been here all along without me knowing they existed, then closed my eyes and let go. It was such a relief, just letting go.

5

THE DISTINGUISHED GUESTS

A strange repeating cry woke me up. It took me a few seconds to realize a rooster was crowing its head off and I was upstairs in Jackie's house somewhere out in the forest in the state of Washington. I peeked at my watch on the nightstand. It was five in the morning, but the room was bright with the rising sun. Go back to sleep? Not if that rooster could help it.

Cody hadn't visited during the night. No doubt the nightlights had helped. Jackie had come up with three: one for his room, one for the hall, and one for the bathroom across from Neal's door.

As for me, no matter that I'd been sleeping in a haven of peace on earth, I'd fought my sheets all night. A ridiculous nightmare had kept me tossing and turning. I was on a sinking ship on the way to Pakistan, no less. Everybody was getting in the lifeboats, but suddenly my brother was missing. Something about going to rescue the dogs in the hold.

Finally I found him, but when we got back to the deck Uncle Neal didn't have any quarters for the life jackets in the vending machines.

Look who's preoccupied with disaster, I thought. And quit renting the movie *Titanic*.

The rooster crowed again, then again and again. Cody, I realized, was standing at the open door watching me wake up. He crossed to the window and said, "I can see that rooster from here. Did it wake you up?"

"Duh." I propped up my head with the extra pillow. I'm charming in the mornings.

At the window, Cody announced that Uncle Neal was in the parking lot moving kennel carriers from the van to the back of an old pickup.

He went to another window. "Jackie's on her way to the barn to milk her goats with the golden retrievers."

All I could do was yawn. "I bet you anything she uses her hands."

"Shannon," Cody groaned. "Wake up! Let's go!"

I humored him. Barefoot and still in my I ♥ NEW YORK sleep shirt, I followed him downstairs and out to the goat barn. Jackie was sitting on a stool, milking a goat. The nanny goat was standing on a platform in front of her and eating grain from a small wooden box. Slats on either side of the nanny's neck kept her from backing her head out. Jackie's hands were amazingly strong and quick. For someone in her sixties who claimed to have enough metal in her body to start a junkyard, she was doing all right. Jackie had told us over supper that she'd been in a terrible car wreck years before. She swerved to avoid a deer and crashed into a tree.

Cody was riveted by the jets of milk shooting into the

pail. Naturally he had to try it, but couldn't get even a dribble to come out. Jackie told him that you have to get the hang of it, to which my brother replied, Cody-fashion: "I've seen bald eagles before, up at the Palisades, but I never heard a rooster crow." He asked if he could collect the eggs, asked if he could bottle-feed the baby raccoons, asked if *he* had to drink goat's milk. Jackie's answers were yes, yes, and no.

The first nanny was done eating her grain and was fidgeting. Jackie quickly finished milking, then released her. The goat jumped off the platform and goat number two took her place. Jackie started talking to us about Uncle Neal, how fond she was of him, at least as much as her sons. Cody got that peculiar expression on his face that means he's just about to ask an inappropriate question. "What happened to *Mister* Jackie?"

Fortunately, Jackie was amused. "You're interested in ancient history, eh? Well, Cody, Mr. Jackie and I split over religious differences. He thought he was God and I didn't."

This was more of an answer than Cody was capable of digesting. It left him speechless. Jackie laughed, then ran her hand over his head. "Ask an honest question," she said, "I'll give you an honest answer."

As Jackie milked the third goat she told us how happy she was that we were going to be staying with her for the summer. When I said that my mother didn't really know much about Neal's situation, she looked at me a little funny. "How do you mean?" she asked.

"I mean, she had no idea he was going to have to find a different place to live when we came. I guess he didn't tell her."

"Oh," Jackie said. "Anything else she doesn't know?"

I couldn't tell what she was getting at. "Probably a lot, I guess. They're both bad about keeping in touch. For another thing, she thought he had all kinds of time on his hands this summer, from being unemployed."

Jackie hesitated, then shrugged and worried her hand through her gray hair. Something was making her uncomfortable. "As much as I appreciate all he does," Jackie said finally, "I wish Neal wouldn't work so much. I keep telling him to take it easy. He needs to take better care of himself. That's one reason I'm so glad he took me up on my suggestion that the three of you live here, with me. I can look after him better here. Maybe he'll even stay after you go— but don't tell him I said that. Okay? You promise?"

Cody nodded uncertainly. I wasn't much closer to understanding why the secrecy. Neal was a grown man and Jackie didn't want to appear to be mothering him even if she sort of was, that's what I thought.

"I want you to know I'm thrilled to have family under my roof again," Jackie said, "and that's how I think of you already."

Back in the kitchen, we watched Jackie strain the milk through a cheesecloth. She asked if we wanted to take a quick tour of her menagerie before she made breakfast for us and Uncle Neal. "Should I change?" I asked. I wasn't really dressed.

Jackie shrugged. "The volunteers won't be showing up this early. How about you, Cody?"

My brother screwed up his face and said, "It depends on what a menagerie is."

"A menagerie is an odd assortment of birds and beasts. Mine numbers over five hundred at the moment. Come on, I'd like you to meet my distinguished guests."

Jackie's opening of the clinic door was greeted by
rustling and chirping. "We're filled to overflowing," Jackie
said. "It's baby season." From floor to ceiling, row upon
row, it was baby bird condos everywhere we looked, small
plastic enclosures with screen doors. Some of the patients
were solo birds and some, babies that must have been
orphaned in the same nest. Two especially adorable yellow
fuzz balls were begging with their necks stretched to the
limit, mouths wide open. "Pigeons," Jackie said.

"You better feed 'em," Cody told her.

"Don't you see the bags under my eyes? I just did, three
hours ago. See the whiteboard on the wall with all the
checklists? That's our system for being sure everybody's
getting fed."

Jackie called out the names of other birds as we walked
by them: "Sparrows, crows, robins, grosbeaks, finches,
swallows, wrens, starlings. Those are baby barn owls. We
have thirty-one of them at the moment. Every patient's little
hospital room is cleaned every day. Food, water, warmth—
we can't let them get chilled. Baby birds are so fragile."

We were turning a corner. The rooms were small, and I
felt a little claustrophobic. I'd pictured the clinic more like
a hospital. This was more like a poorly designed house. A
large bird began to cry fiercely from the next section.
"Birds of prey, kids. Raptors are so magnificent!"

The cages along this wall were much larger. "We have
four kinds of owls at the moment, three species of hawks—
that's the red-tailed. Here's the osprey that's been doing all
the yelling, here's another osprey. They're fish hunters.
These two are brother and sister. The male was badly
burned—look at his poor feathers. Their parents built their
nest on top of a light pole at a racetrack. There was a short

circuit and the nest caught fire. That's a kestrel; here's a golden eagle from clear over near Spokane. It has a severe infection from a leg-hold trap, which the voters have outlawed. We've had a lot of luck with raptors, so they keep coming. We're the biggest raptor-rehab place in the state."

We passed by a room banked with sinks, counters, cabinets and refrigerators, with a long table down its center. "Food prep," Jackie said. Everything was clean, but nothing was new. The place looked like it had been stocked from garage sales.

A peek at the laundry and we turned a corner. We were into the small mammals. The patients here were squirrels, possums and weasels, full-grown raccoons, our baby raccoons, and a darling baby porcupine. The baby beaver in the bathtub was cuter yet. It was love at first sight for Cody, who dropped to his knees at the edge of the tub. The beaver couldn't have been more than fifteen inches long, adorable flat tail included. It came to Cody, scratching at the enamel with its tiny claws.

"Will it bite?" Cody asked. I hoped not; they were practically nose to nose.

"They're gentle," Jackie told him. "Go ahead and pick him up."

"You're kidding."

"Go ahead, pick him up."

Cody did just that, put it against his chest. This was love. They touched noses. "If Mom and Dad could only see this," I cooed. "If Uncle Neal could—"

"Neal never comes into the clinic," Jackie said.

"He doesn't? How come?"

She shrugged. "He says, 'I bring 'em, you fix 'em.'"

The little beaver gripped one of Cody's fingers in its little hands. Cody looked up and said, "What's wrong with him?"

"He's an orphan, that's all. Some homeowners didn't like it that beavers moved into *their* stream and started taking down *their* trees. When they killed the beavers, this little guy was overlooked. So much ignorance, so much education left to be done. The best water engineer in creation is that little creature in your hands, Cody. Beavers would have built those people ponds, then all sorts of birds would have come, not to mention frogs, fish, crawdads, turtles . . . All they ever had to do to save their trees was wrap them waist-high with chicken wire. Cody, you can put him back now."

Reluctantly, Cody did, and asked, "Does he have a name?"

"No, but you can give him one," Jackie said as we turned another corner. The clinic went off in all directions like the word lines on a Scrabble board. You could tell Jackie had put the place together in bits and pieces as she got donations, with volunteer labor from the slapped-together looks of it.

"Chuckie," Cody proclaimed. "I'll call him Chuckie."

"Good name," Jackie said, throwing open yet another door that said MEDICAL RECOVERY ROOM.

There was Uncle Neal, sitting by a carrier on a table in the middle of the room. Sage was at his feet. We'd just heard that Neal didn't come inside the clinic. The look on Jackie's face, well, she couldn't have been more surprised.

On the bottom of the carrier, plopped on its belly on a layer of shredded newspaper, was the fledgling eagle that had fallen out of the nest in the park. Jackie was still in shock at seeing Neal there. Neal was all serious as he looked up at Jackie. "She's not doing so well, is she?"

"Both wings had to be pinned," Jackie said measuredly. "That's quite an operation for a very delicate, very young, very wild creature. Eagles can fly with pins in their wing bones. It all depends on how much movement the injury will allow. For now, she's on antibiotics. Time will tell. I'm even more worried that there's so little fight in her."

"She's been fed?"

"We tube-fed her last night after the operation and we will again as soon as Rosie comes in. Her medicine is mixed in with the food. Neal, I'm heading back to make breakfast. Would you take the kids to see the outdoor pens and bring them right back so they can get dressed and down for breakfast?"

6

DON'T WORRY,
YOU CAN TRUST ME

Uncle Neal pulled himself away from the pathetic-looking eagle and took us outside. We raced through the center's rehab environments: there were pens, runs, various ramshackle plywood buildings, big flying enclosures. We missed quite a few of the distinguished guests in the outdoor area, but we saw raccoons, possums, cottontail rabbits, baby skunks, river otters, and birds of prey, including eleven bald eagles, five kinds of hawks, and a trio of great horned owls. We were about to run down a path that led into the farthest corner of the rehab area when Neal called after us, "I don't think Jackie wants us down there. The coyotes and deer are supposed to see people as little as possible."

We looked in on a water theme park for geese, ducks, herons, cranes, and a trumpeter swan. We stared at a full-grown mountain lion named Sasha—a permanent resident—pacing inside her well-padlocked chain-link enclosure. Her pen had three big sections for her to roam around in. The cougar stopped pacing, bared her fangs, and hissed at us. I mean, she was six or seven feet from head to tail. I shrank back, and Cody about jumped out of his skin.

Through a peephole in a large corral of solid plywood, we spotted a bear cub, a living teddy bear. A black bear, Neal said it was. The cub lived in a chain-link enclosure with multiple rooms like the cougar's. On account of the plywood blind, it couldn't see any other animals, or people coming and going. It had a den of sorts inside a stack of hay bales, wooden platforms to play on, and a tree to climb, but it couldn't see out except for the sky above a ceiling of metal mesh. "Poor bear," I said. "It's in solitary confinement."

"This is making me sad," Cody told his uncle.

"I know how you feel," Neal said, "but if it's ever going to be wild, it can't get comfortable around humans. Otherwise it would be a dead bear soon after it was released."

The cub was batting around a stick, running after it, tumbling over a log, sitting on its haunches. "Watch," Neal said. "See that door swinging open, the one attached to the clinic? Here comes Big Bear."

It was hard to get a good look through the peepholes. A full-grown bear on the path between the plywood fence and the chain-link pen was walking along with a bowl in its hands. "Wait a second," Cody said indignantly. "That's somebody in a bear suit. Look at the gloves."

"Forgot to mention," Uncle Neal said with a smile. "That's Rosie, the clinic manager."

Big Bear got down on her hands and knees, entered a section of the pen closed off to the cub. She set out the food, left, then pulled on a rope that hoisted a door like a guillotine. The cub hesitated at the opening, stood up sniffing, then came on through for its food.

We passed back through the clinic and were going out the front door when we ran smack into the wild-haired boy I'd spotted the night before, the one about my age. He was on his way inside.

I don't know who was the most surprised. I'm sure I was the most embarrassed, in my nightshirt.

Neal snapped, "What are you doing here, Tyler?"

"I thought somebody would be here," he said, looking at Uncle Neal, then at me in my nightshirt, then away. He was really embarrassed too.

"It's early," Neal said. "Real early." My uncle was very unhappy.

"I thought someone was *always* here."

Jackie must have seen this boy, this Tyler, from the kitchen window. She joined us, looking all concerned.

"I was just going to do my four hours early today," Tyler explained. "I walked here, if you're wondering. I'll start cleaning cages. Don't worry, you can trust me."

I sneaked a good look at him. He looked like he'd slept in his clothes, or maybe not slept at all.

"I can't trust you to do a good job on an empty stomach," Jackie said, and that's how Tyler joined us for breakfast.

At breakfast he didn't say much. In, fact he didn't say anything at all. Neither did I. I was fully dressed by then, but still embarrassed.

Tyler kept his eyes down on his omelet. It was a strange breakfast, everybody off-balance, maybe not such a good idea. In the silences you heard everybody chewing and swallowing. The kitchen faucet had a slow drip. Cody was in agony, wanting out, but wasn't saying a thing. Finally he distracted himself by dangling a piece of sausage at the side of his chair. Other than me, only Sage noticed. It wasn't the first time Cody had tried to win her over with food, but Sage didn't budge from the corner of the room.

Tyler ate ravenously even though he'd protested that he'd eaten at home. His cheeks were ruddy, maybe from feeling self-conscious. He'd visited the bathroom and washed up, arranged his thick dark hair somehow, but he still looked like a wild creature who'd just come in from the woods. I couldn't help but wonder what his home life must be like and why he was at Jackie's in the first place. Something told me I didn't really want the answers.

7

LATE-BREAKING NEWS

I was folding and sorting my clothes. I had a lot of them to put away. It felt good to take a little time, settle in, and enjoy the scents that the breeze brought through the open window. Jackie had flower beds everywhere, and blooming rhododendrons lined her long driveway.

I already liked it out here in the woods. I loved my room, not fancy but clean and airy and fresh with the fragrance of the nearby cedars. I liked Jackie's house, I liked her home-baked bread, I liked her.

So far, so good. We'd landed safely and so had my parents. First thing after breakfast Jackie had let me check my e-mail from her office computer. "The adventure begins," my mother reported. They'd made it to Karachi, Pakistan.

On the spot, I got on the keys. They had said they would check their e-mail before leaving for Islamabad and Peshawar. I filled them in on our adventures so far. Were they ever going to be surprised.

Uncle Neal was away, dropping the van at a repair place. Cody was in the clinic with Chuckie and some other new friends. Jackie had said he could pull some carrots from the garden, clean and dice them for the baby skunks, and he might like to help Rosie make a fruit dish for the baby porcupine.

It was good to have a chance to catch my breath and gather my thoughts. I found myself thinking about Tyler, the hurt in his voice when he said, "Don't worry, you can trust me." Why *wouldn't* they trust him?

Tyler had acted distant after breakfast when I'd run into him in the clinic. He was cleaning cages. The nightshirt episode and the awkwardness at breakfast were fresh, and he looked away. I was about to do the same when I realized how strange it was going to be if we couldn't even be around each other, talk, and generally act normal. I said something about how great it was that there were so many volunteers at Jackie's. It was meant as an offhanded compliment. He looked at me and said in a wounded sort of way, "Well, yeah, but I'm not exactly volunteering."

I decided not to ask what he meant.

I was almost finished hanging my clothes in the closet when Cody came flying upstairs with late-breaking news:

1) Uncle Neal had a bumper sticker on the back of his old truck that said VERY FUNNY, SCOTTY, NOW BEAM DOWN MY CLOTHES.

2) Another one said FRIENDS DON'T LET FRIENDS EAT FARMED SALMON.

3) Uncle Neal said it was hard to drive and keep an eye out for new bumper stickers, so Cody could help out with that.

4) Rosie said Sage didn't like kids under a certain size because a little kid had been really mean to her when she was a puppy.

5) Rosie has a son named Robbie who is seven, too. Jackie is a "midgewife" and delivered Robbie when he was born.

6) Jackie was going to show Cody how to collect the eggs from the henhouse. You had to stand up to the rooster but you couldn't hit him with anything or kick him because you might break his leg.

7) The baby porcupine and the baby skunks are almost as cool as Chuckie. He got to help with bottle feeding—it was major the way Chuckie tugged on the bottle. The baby skunks don't even stink.

8) When he asked a couple of people about Tyler, they acted like they were busy.

After that last item, my little brother looked at me funny. I said, "How come you were asking people about Tyler?"

"I thought you'd want to know," he replied sheepishly.

"Cody, all kinds of people help out here. Close to a hundred every week this time of year, Jackie said. They come and go all day."

"Half of the animals die," Cody blurted out, hurt in his voice, on his face.

"Who told you that?"

"Tyler did. He said some of them get put to sleep. The bodies get taken away and cremated."

Before I could say a thing, my little brother turned and ran. Cody bounded down the stairs yelling, "Jackie's going to take us to see some low-flying fish!"

8

UNDERGROUND WITH
A TOUGH CUSTOMER

Cody was right, Jackie had plans for us. She drove us straight into downtown Seattle. We parked under a viaduct across from where people drove on and off the ferries. Next thing I knew we were strolling along Alaskan Way, the street closest to the water. A pier full of tourist traps caught my eye, and we started browsing.

In the very first shop, Cody found himself a color poster of Mount Saint Helens erupting. A conch shell, a candy bar, and a plastic tarantula later, he had maxed his weekly allowance. I was the treasurer and warned him there wouldn't be any advances. "I'm a grasshopper, not an ant," he declared. Cody suffered through another hour of browsing until we climbed the steps to Seattle's famous Pike Place Market. He was in search of the low-flying fish Jackie had advertised, whatever they were.

Pike Place was spilling over with tourists. The first section we entered was an open-air flower market, a riot of exotic fragrances. I would have bought an arrangement of dahlias for Jackie if she wasn't up to her ears in flowers at home and I hadn't spent $14 on a Seattle photo calendar. A woman speaking an Asian language was weeding seconds from the bulk flowers and tossing them under the table. She saw me standing there sort of blissfully, sort of wishfully. She smiled and presented me with a beautiful orchid. I said thanks, turned around, and slipped its stem through a buttonhole in Jackie's blouse.

The appeal of the flower section escaped Cody. Our grasshopper dragged us through the vegetable section and ever closer to the strong smell of seafood. We were soon surrounded by crab, squid, and octopus. The fish came next, iced down and on display. "Where are the low-flying fish?" Cody fretted, craning his neck. "That's the whole reason I came."

Jackie didn't look hopeful. "Maybe they aren't flying today."

Up ahead, foot traffic had come to a standstill. One particular stall was mobbed. We heard cheers, shouts, and laughing. I caught Cody's attention and pointed to a sign suspended above the crowd: CAUTION —LOW-FLYING FISH. Just then Cody saw one, an airborne salmon longer than his arm. I hoisted him up so he could see better. As soon as a customer bought a fish, one of the workers grabbed it and tossed it across the stall to others who did the wrapping. They never dropped one.

"This is *major*," Cody said.

As they were wrapping a sockeye salmon for Jackie, the cell phone in her purse rang. I fished it out and answered for her. It was Neal, and he wanted to know if his assistants were available for a rescue. He said it was Cody's chance to see Pioneer Square, where the bricks had fallen off the buildings during the earthquake.

I asked Neal where he was calling from and he said, "From the Filipino eats place."

I said, "Where's that?"

"Right across from you," he said, "about fifty feet away."

I looked across the street, and there was Neal's shiny head and smiling face amid the crowd.

A few minutes later Jackie was on her way home with dinner and we were on our way to Pioneer Square in Neal's rusty old Toyota pickup. It was challenging fitting the three of us and Sage into the cab of the toy-sized truck. With Cody in the middle and Sage propping her front feet on the dash, we managed.

We were barely under way when Cody grinned and said, "Very funny Scotty, now beam down my clothes. Friends don't let friends eat farmed salmon."

Neal winked and said, "Friends don't let friends drive naked."

Cody chortled like a pig in deep mud. I gave Uncle Neal a glance to the effect of, Don't go there.

Pioneer Square was ringed by five- and six-story buildings with a small leafy park in the middle. A carrier in one hand and big fishing net in the other, flak-jacketed partner at his side, Neal was quite a camera magnet. "My uncle, the tourist attraction," I kidded him.

"Let's keep moving," he said under his breath. We hustled past boutiques, coffeehouses, and bookstores. Pioneer Square felt familiar, a lot like Greenwich Village in New York, though the totem pole in the middle of the square reminded me I was a long way from home.

We stopped at the door of something called Seattle's

Famous Underground Tours, and were they ever happy to see us. They'd had to cancel two tours after a raccoon got into the underground, whatever that was.

A man led us to a spot where he opened a door fronting an alley, then shut it behind us as we descended into the late nineteenth century. "*Tidnab*," Neal announced on the way down the stairs. Suddenly his dog was on high alert. Uncle Neal put on the heavy coat he'd been carrying over his arm and pulled on a pair of welding gloves.

We found ourselves looking into musty shops and stores as we walked along streets abandoned long ago. "We're under Pioneer Square right now," Uncle Neal whispered. "Keep your voices down so we don't scare the raccoon into some deep corner."

The main route that the tourists followed on their tours was lit dimly by electric light. I probed with Neal's powerful flashlight beam into dark nooks and crannies. "We wouldn't have a chance of finding that Bandit-spelled-backwards without Sage," Cody whispered to Neal.

"You got that right. I can't believe you figured out the raccoon code word so fast."

"Beam me up, Scotty. Why did they have to stop the tours?"

"They were afraid of getting sued. Afraid the raccoon might get cornered and rip some tourist's face off."

A few steps farther and the flashlight beam lit up a strange sight: a toilet mounted on a platform about six feet off the ground, with a ladder leading up to it.

"Explain, Uncle Neal," I whispered. Cody slapped his hand to his mouth to keep from laughing.

"Sure. When Seattle first got started, this part of town was built on the tidal flats. Whenever the tide came in, they had a problem. Everything backed up and the sewage flowed the wrong direction. When they got a strong high tide—*whoosh*—exploding toilets! Kind of like Old Faithful in Yellowstone Park. You didn't want to be in the wrong place at the wrong time—you get the idea."

Cody pumped his fist. "Got it!"

"That's gross," I protested. "Certifiably."

"But Shan doesn't mind," Cody said. "Keep going, Uncle Neal."

"Well, all they could do was build the toilets up in the air, like the one you're looking at. Afterward, you came down the ladder and washed up. There's the washbasin, on ground level. Isn't history wonderful?"

"This is the ultimate," Cody said.

"Cody, let me tell you why the great fire of 1889 wasn't such a disaster after all. After the fire, the city fathers, in their wisdom, decided to rebuild this whole part of town twelve feet higher."

Cody laughed through his fingers. "So the sewage would go downhill."

"That's right. Gravity isn't just a good idea, it's the law. They built on the old foundations, then raised the streets to match the top of the old first story. While they were rebuilding, you had to climb a ladder from the sidewalk to get onto the street. You crossed the street, then climbed down a ladder to get to the sidewalk on the other side. I kid you not."

Uncle Neal suddenly put a forefinger to his lips, took the flashlight, and pointed it through a ragged break in one of the stone walls. Far down an ancient alley, a pair of eyes shone weirdly in the dark.

"How did you know?" I whispered. "Did Sage tell you?"

"Indeed she did. Adult raccoon. That *tidnab* is gonna be a tough customer."

The border collie was twitching all over, yet when Uncle Neal gave the word, she didn't bolt. Sage stalked slowly into the darkness, the hair along her spine standing on end.

Uncle Neal brandished his salmon net. "Give me lots of swinging room. Let's stand well off to the side so we aren't blocking the raccoon's way out."

Before long Sage was barking, the raccoon was growling and hissing, and there was a nasty scuffle going on. "Sage knows how to use her flak jacket," Neal said. "I just hope she has enough light to see by."

A couple minutes later the raccoon popped out, but not where we were expecting. Barking wildly, Sage flushed it out half a block behind us. Neal took off at a gallop with the flashlight and the net. I followed with the carrier.

The raccoon kept trying to get off the street into the doorways and shadows. Every time, Sage leaped in front and turned it back. Now it was caught between Sage and Neal. Uncle Neal made his move. Quick as could be, he had the raccoon trapped under his net.

Now came the trick: how to get this snarling, hissing, spitting beastie into the carrier.

The raccoon delivered a number of vicious bites on Neal's welding gloves and the sleeves of his heavy coat. At last, when Neal let go, the raccoon practically leaped the rest of the way into the carrier. We were out of there.

Fifteen minutes later, Uncle Neal released the raccoon where the Duwamish River meets Elliott Bay. "Stay out of downtown, you hear?"

As we headed home, Cody started fretting about the salmon Jackie had picked up for dinner. "Is she going to cook it like fish and chips?" he asked hopefully.

Neal winced. "Fresh salmon, deep fried in batter?"

Just then Neal's cell phone rang. It was Jackie with a proposition for Cody. If he didn't mind the quick turn-around when we got home, Rosie's husband was going to come by to take him and Robbie to a baseball game. The Mariners were playing the New York Yankees, and Robbie was planning on hot dogs at the ballpark.

The kid must have been born under a lucky star.

9

FLYING GRAVEL

The first day of July, Neal's bald eagle was moved outdoors to a private pen, one of the large flying enclosures. Inside of all that space she was going to live in a wire cage lined with shredded newspaper. At least she'd be in the open air and could see the sky. Neal thought it might help. The eagle still hadn't stood up.

Every chance Neal got he was there with her. He'd talk softly to her, tell her to hold on, tell her to fight, to live. The big fledgling just lay in a heap on the floor of her cage. On his last visit of the day he would throw a blanket over her cage so she wouldn't get chilled. I couldn't help wondering why he'd gotten so attached to this bird, especially after Jackie's remark about him not liking to get involved with the rehab part of the operation.

The van was back from the shop. Making the rounds was easier after a week crowded into Neal's Toyota. The rescues were usually of small birds and mammals injured by cats, dogs, and cars. My job was to keep up with the pager, return calls on the cell phone, and take directions. We collected dozens of baby squirrels that had fallen out of their nests, a juvenile possum that might have fallen off its mother's back, a fuzzy duckling whose tiny leg had been accidentally broken by an eight-year-old boy. People would notice the lettering across the side of the ambulance and the seal-and-eagle logo. Lots would smile, give us a thumbs-up. But a few would frown—go figure—or actually give us a thumbs-down.

We and Neal's eagle had been at the center two weeks when the vet came back to look at a new set of X rays. Cody and I were there when Uncle Neal got the news. Dr. Minorca was my mother's age and reminded me of her on the job, professional yet still a regular person.

"I wish I could tell you she might fly one day," Dr. Minorca told him. She looked at Jackie, then back to Neal. "Unfortunately, it's not to be. The right wing is healing fine, but the left one never will. It was just too bad a break. I'm sorry."

"Such a shame," Jackie said.

Uncle Neal grimly said, "I just hope she's going to live."

The vet replied with a shrug, then added, "I sure don't like it that she's not feeding on her own. That she's not even standing up worries me especially. She might just throw in the towel. Time will tell."

"Liberty's going to make it," my uncle said with conviction. "I know she will."

"So you've given her a name?" The vet sounded like maybe that wasn't such a good idea.

"After Liberty Place, the street Shannon and Cody live on, in Weehawken, New Jersey. Not to mention she's the symbol of our country."

After the bad news, Uncle Neal's devotion to the bird only

grew. He would talk-talk-talk to Liberty, and try to feed her
small fish or bits of beef heart. "It's okay, Liberty," I heard
him say, "It's okay if you never fly It's okay, it's okay." The
big fledgling would look at him, and she'd take food sometimes, but she wouldn't stand up.

Another week went by, and Liberty was still a sack of
potatoes. One day in the clinic I asked Jackie what her
chances were. "Neal picked a tough case," she answered.
"That bird's eyes are dull, and that's never a good sign.
She's got to have something to live for. She might have a
chance if she bonds with Neal. Thing is, bald eagles nor-
mally want nothing to do with humans. They go to great
lengths to get away from them."

I went to Liberty's pen in search of Uncle Neal but found
Tyler there instead. He was inside the pen holding Liberty
while Rosie slid the feeding tube through her mouth and
down her esophagus. Tyler looked up at me when I came in,
kind of like an old friend. He was proud to be holding the
eagle.

I couldn't help feeling warm and fuzzy about Tyler. I
mean, he looked so happy holding that magnificent bird.
Actually, the feeling had been growing slowly since the first
day. We would bump into each other, talk a little, not about
anything in particular, just kind of Hi, how are you—keeping it light but basically trying out being friends. He'd smile
when he'd see me, and a smile looked good on him. He had
a beautiful smile, in fact. I seemed to be the only one around
the place he could talk to.

Just then Uncle Neal showed up. He looked anything but
happy about Tyler holding Liberty. Neal didn't say anything,
just looked very stressed out until Rosie and Tyler left the
area.

"So what's the deal with Tyler?" I asked. Tyler was a topic

nobody seemed to bring up, including me, but now I wanted
to know more.

"What is it you want to know?"

"I mean, what's he doing here?"

"Nobody's told you? Jackie? Rosie?"

"They could tell I didn't want to know. I guess I'm ready
to hear it."

Neal breathed out, breathed in. "Okay, sure. Tyler's on
probation. From juvenile court. One of the things Jackie
does here, besides working with the animals, is help kids
who've gotten into trouble. Sometimes the court will let
them do community service, like working at the center,
instead of time in a detention center. Tyler's judge assigned
him to work here four hours a day."

"So that's why he told me wasn't exactly a volunteer."

"I'd like to know what he is, 'exactly.' Jackie's had a lot of
success with some of these kids, really turned their lives
around, but this time . . . Well, I think she's over her head.
I just don't think she should risk it. If he's going to be
around the animals at all, then he should stay in the clinic
cleaning cages. Where people can keep an eye on him."

"What in the world did he do that makes you so worried?"

Uncle Neal swallowed hard. "Cruelty to animals. And I
don't mean he forgot to feed a pet."

Just that quick, I held up my hand, as if to ward off a
blow. "Stop," I said. "Don't tell me any more than that."

I took off for a walk into the heart of Jackie's tall cedars,
a good place to air out my head. All the same I couldn't quit
thinking about Tyler. Maybe I should've asked for the
details, but I truly didn't want to know, didn't want to have
those kinds of pictures inside my head.

I needed to be alone. I climbed up and onto an old stump

about six feet above the ground. The day was hot, but inside
the trees it was nice and cool. The stump was so far across
that I was able to lie on my back, stretch my arms and legs
wide, and still be contained within its circle. I looked up
through the branches at a tiny patch of blue high above and
got real sad about all the cruelty in the world, all the
wounded people. My mind jumped to the refugee camp in
Pakistan. I hadn't heard from my parents since they got
there, and that was scary.

Don't go there, I thought, don't brood on all the bad
things that could happen. You promised you wouldn't. I
concentrated on relaxing, on how nice the breeze was, how
beautiful the light filtering through the trees, and I nodded
off.

I woke to kid voices filtering through the cedar boughs. I
couldn't make out the words, but I could tell it was Cody
and his friend Robbie. I climbed down off the stump and
edged out of the cedar grove toward their voices.

They were playing with the garden hose outside Jackie's
garden, which was fenced against the wild deer and her own
goats. The nannies were grazing close by but not near
enough that Cody could spray them with the hose. The
goats were not interested in playing, and they hated getting
wet. The golden retrievers watched from the shade of a big
maple.

Cody and Robbie were packing dirt. It was fun peeking
into their world. They were making a dam. It was pond
construction, your standard little boy water engineering
project.

I left the trees and crossed to the garden gate, then crept
closer down the garden's center path. The pole beans and
the dill made excellent cover. When I reached the raspberry

patch I could hear every word. The topic was Chuckie.

It wasn't until I sat, pulled my knees up to my chest, and peeked through the vines that I figured out that the baby beaver was actually there. They were making a pond for him. Chuckie was swimming back and forth in the rising water like a motorized toy, only he was alive.

"Wait a minute," Cody was saying, "Chuckie should be making his own dam."

"Let's tear out this dirt dam and start making a new one out of sticks and mud," Robbie said. "Then he'll get the idea."

With the pond emptying fast, Chuckie quit swimming and looked around quizzically. "It's just for a few minutes," Robbie explained.

The waters were soon rising again, but so far Chuckie hadn't pitched in to help with the construction. The retrievers saw the little beaver swimming around, came over, and sniffed at it. Cody ordered them off. "Don't even think about it!"

The goldens went back to the shade and lay down.

Robbie said, "How come you like Sage better than them? They play stick with you and she won't."

"They're too easy. Sage is smart and knows how to rescue animals. I wish she'd get to like me."

"Don't you wish we could play with the bear cub, Cody?"

"That would be major, but he'd bite us. He's too wild. I like to peek through the hole in the fence, but usually Tyler's there watching him."

Tyler's name hit me like a bucket of cold water. They went back to their dam project, and I slipped out the other gate and into the parking lot. And there he was, the very person I would have gone out of my way to avoid right then.

"Waiting for someone?" I asked Tyler, my heart thumping a little faster than usual.

"My dad. He's picking me up."

I started to walk away.

"Hey, what's going on?" Tyler called. "What's the deal? Did you hear something bad about me from your uncle?"

"Not really," I said. "I don't want to talk about it."

"Okay, fine, I understand not talking about stuff. But what's the deal with Cody?"

"What do you mean by that?"

"Well, he kind of steers a wide path around me. Is it something I said?"

I had half a second to think if I was going to disguise my feelings, but I hated that sort of thing. "Well, yeah," I said. "It was something you said, right after we got here."

"You're kidding."

"I guess if you really want to know, it was that stuff you told him about half of the animals dying, getting euthanized and cremated and all. It hurt his feelings. Was that really necessary?"

Tyler flushed. "So you *are* upset with me. Well, he was asking. I'm sorry, but it's true."

"You didn't have to be so *negative*, Tyler. He's just a little kid. Neal says you were exaggerating, but even if it's true, you could have talked about the ones that make it."

"He's a great kid, Shannon. I'm sorry." Tyler ran his hand through his unruly hair, hung his head. "I'm real sorry." His hands went into the bottom of his pockets. He looked down the driveway.

I was surprised to hear him sounding so sincere, surprised he had it in him to say he was sorry.

Now I was confused. This was the Tyler I'd seen with

Liberty. But what about the Tyler Neal described, the one so vicious a judge was making him pay for what he'd done?

Tyler was reaching out to me, asking me to believe in him, trust him. I couldn't walk away. I had felt it from the first, his need to be understood. Not by everybody, by me. Wasn't it true what my parents believed, that it's up to everybody to help in the healing of the world?

If I was going to even try, I had to try to get past not wanting to know the bad stuff. "Tyler, is it true what they say, about you hurting animals?"

He didn't say anything, just nodded grimly.

Part of me wanted to get away from him, part of me wanted to stay.

"One animal," he added. "I don't suppose that helps any."

Cautiously, I said, "Maybe it's none of my business, but is anyone helping you? I mean, like are you getting counseling or anything?"

"Yeah," he said. "I am. Lots of talking, a couple times a week. Hey, can we just drop it, okay? All I want is to finish up here and not blow it. The way people look at me, like your uncle, it gives me the creeps."

"What about Jackie?" I asked. "She's trying to help, isn't she?"

He laughed. "She's wacky, in case you haven't noticed."

"What do you mean? Why would you say that?"

"I mean, I like her and all, but don't you think she's mental? A lot of these animals, maybe most of them—squirrels, possums, pigeons, crows, skunks—I mean, give me a break. They're mostly pests. Why all this effort? It's crazy."

A car turned off the pavement and was rumbling up the gravel driveway. With all the trees, it wasn't in sight yet. "Quick," Tyler said, "duck behind those bushes."

Tyler was pointing at Jackie's thick hedge of rhododendrons along the drive. I looked at him like he was crazy.
"Just do it!" he yelled

I don't know why, but I did what I was told. I ran behind
the hedge and sat there motionless, peering through the
dense foliage.

I didn't see much, just a glimpse of a dark-haired, red-
faced man as he jerked his boat of a sedan around in the
narrow driveway. It took three tries. He was driving angry,
lurching the car forward and then back as if he couldn't get
out of Jackie's fast enough. Finally he had the car pointed
back down the driveway. Tyler jumped in and his father hit
the accelerator hard, spraying gravel all around.

I understood a lot more than I had a minute before.

10

BABY SQUIRRELS
AND BAD HISTORY

I woke up scared that night. Not hearing from my parents was more worrisome than I'd been admitting. We hadn't heard anything since they left Islamabad, bound for the refugee camp in Peshawar. I'd kept up a stream of e-mails but nothing was coming back. Had Pakistan just swallowed them up? Right after Tyler left down the driveway with his father I'd done some e-mailing back and forth with Doctors Without Borders. They were working on getting me in touch, but what if something awful had happened?

The big red numbers on the nightstand clock said 1:14. In the next room, Cody was talking in his sleep. The kid needed a dump truck to unload his head. I threw my robe on over my nightshirt and tiptoed to his open door.

Cody's head was at the foot of his bed, while his feet had a firm grasp on his pillow. His blankie was wrapped around his face, maybe to break the glare from the nightlight in the hall. He was mumbling away, but now and again I could catch what he was saying, including "Got it!" "Hang on!" "Major!" and "Good, Sage."

Cody's hand reached out, flicked the blankie from his face. He pushed something away, said "Back off!" Obviously he wasn't talking to the border collie anymore. Maybe the retrievers were all over him with their sticky tennis ball.

More mumbling, then a minute later, "Let go of those skunks!"

I could go back to sleep now, at least try.

As I was turning the corner into my room, the light downstairs went on. No doubt Jackie had gotten up to do a feeding. She'd been bringing the baby squirrels over for the night. They had to be fed every three hours.

At the foot of the stairs I could hear faint mewing from two plastic laundry tubs on the coffee table. I peeked inside. The squirrels were sorted by age: the tiny ones with eyes still shut in one tub, the ones that were a little larger, with more fur and eyes opened, in the other. Almost all were squirming in their rumpled towel bedding.

Jackie spotted me from the stove, where she was heating formula. "Hi there. Can't sleep?"

"Not really. Could you use some help?"

"Sure could, but don't make a habit of it, Shannon. Being able to sleep is a godsend. I wish your uncle could."

"You mean he doesn't?"

"Snatches a little now and then."

"I never hear anything from his room."

"Sometimes it's because he isn't there. He and his partner glide out of here like a pair of wolves."

"To do what?"

"Prowl the greater Seattle area. Neal parks the van downhill so he can coast down the driveway before he starts the motor. Rosie calls him the Midnight Rambler."

"What a sneak. What's he doing?"

"Rescuing animals, of course."

"But it's dark."

"He's got Sage. At night it's mostly raccoons that get injured on the road, that sort of thing. In the winter, they do it in the dark *and* the rain. He's a nut. He's devoted."

"Maybe a tad bit crazy?"

"Neal can't stand the idea of an animal suffering with a people-related injury and people not trying to help. Believe me, I've tried to talk him out of 24/7. Neal says he can't sleep anyway, might as well be doing what he loves to do. I can't fire him. He's not exactly working for me. We're more like dance partners."

"Was he doing his Midnight Rambler thing even before he was laid off by Boeing?"

Jackie nodded, but she also flinched. There was some sort of conflict in her eyes, but it didn't look like she was going to explain. I said, "You learn something every day around here."

"Never a dull moment. You're really getting to like your uncle, aren't you?"

"I really am. You know, before we came, and early on, I was so anxious about this summer. Maybe I'm still a little nervous, but I'll never be sorry we came."

"And you're crazy about your little brother. He's a real original."

I giggled. "Yeah, I love him to death, the little doof."

Jackie pulled the formula off the stove. "I'm glad I got the chance to know you, Shannon. You have the eyes of a hawk and the heart of a lion."

"Not even—"

"Yes, you do."

"I just wish I'd hear from my parents. It's been three weeks, and I can't stop thinking about all the terrible things that could have happened to them."

"Don't let your imagination get away from you, Shannon. If they were missing, someone would have contacted us. Their e-mails just aren't getting through, that's all."

"Their palm gizmo mustn't work, or there's no phones. That's the thing, I don't even know where they are. Yesterday afternoon I tracked down a way to e-mail Doctors Without Borders. They told me they'd get a message through. Why didn't I think of that before?"

We sat side by side on the living room couch and fed baby squirrels one at a time. It was as simple as cradling one in your left hand and very gently applying pressure to the syringe in your right. At the business end the syringe had a tiny nipple. Before I knew it, I had calmed down.

My first squirrel was nursing contentedly. It looked so innocent, so adorable with its tiny hands and tiny face and big eyes. I thought of Tyler and how dumb he would think this was. "Do you mind if I ask you a question, Jackie?"

"Not a bit. Let's talk when we can. It's always such a circus around the clinic, with the volunteers and all, and you're gone so much of the time with Neal. Oh, half a cc if their eyes are closed, one cc if they're open. Watch carefully. Overfeed 'em and they die on you."

"Got it. . . . The man who roared up the driveway, picked up Tyler, and roared off . . . that's his father, right?"

"Cor-rect," Jackie said, after a slow intake of breath. "Most of the time, Tyler walks. He lives a couple miles up the road. His father picks him up when there's something he wants Tyler to do."

"What does his father do for a living? Scare people?"

"Did he scare you?"

"Well, yeah. I can tell he scares Tyler, too. We were talking in the driveway today and Tyler yells, 'Jump behind the bushes.' That's pretty extreme. Then I saw the guy. *Scary* is as good a word to describe him as any. He looked angry. He looked mean."

Each of us had an empty tub at our feet. We were both done with our first squirrel and set them down in their bedding.

"Well, Shannon, it's like this. Gary Tucker is not exactly the number one fan of Jackie's Wild Seattle. Every time he comes here it makes his blood boil. The years come and go and he hates me as much as ever, hates this place, hates everything the center and I stand for."

"Alrighty, then. You don't beat around the bush, Jackie."

"Life's too short."

Here's what I found out as we fed the squirrels:

1) Tyler's father had wanted the land Jackie's center is on. He's a mechanic, and he needed more land to expand his shop space and park more vehicles.

2) Jackie first started the center in her garage and backyard in north Seattle. Before long she needed more space, lots of space.

3) Jackie made a better offer on the land and Tyler's dad lost out. He was fried because Jackie had money that was donated from a small family foundation, while he had to *work* for a living.

4) Tyler's dad tried to get the town of Cedar Glen and the county to stop the sale of the five acres to Jackie because the wildlife would cause a public health problem.

5) The town and the county liked what Jackie wanted to do with the land. She could give wildlife programs to school groups and 4-H and so on.

6) Tyler's dad got even madder because he was from Cedar Glen, born and raised, and Jackie was an outsider.

7) Years later, now that the probation department and the judge had arranged for his son to do his community service with Jackie, Gary Tucker was all riled up again.

"I knew it would stir up all that bad history," Jackie said. "That's the last thing I wanted. Believe me, I can do with less stress in my life. I told the judge all about Tyler's dad and me, but he still wanted to give it a try. Working here has done a lot of good for a lot of teenagers over the years."

"Had any of them been involved in cruelty to animals?"

"A couple others. The judge, the probation department, his therapist—everyone agreed that working here was exactly the therapy Tyler needed. Theoretically, it should help a lot: taking care of injured animals, helping them, getting to know them, feeling compassion for them."

"I guess I finally have to know what it was Tyler did."

"He broke a dog's back, then drowned the dog in the creek. Fortunately, somebody saw him."

I winced. I tried to think of something to say but came up empty. It was as bad as I was afraid it was going to be.

Jackie waited me out. Finally I said, "You're not sure that working here is helping, are you?"

Jackie shook her head as she reached for another baby squirrel. "It's just that Tyler's been here long enough already. There should be some positive signs in the way he relates to the animals. He keeps himself so stiff, so detached, and not just when he's cleaning cages. I mean, even when he's bottle feeding Chuckie and the little porcupine. I thought for sure they would melt his heart."

"He was pretty pleased with himself, holding Liberty."

"That's hopeful, but I think it doesn't count."

"Why not?"

"He knew you were watching, Shannon. After all, you're a very attractive girl. The look you saw was probably more about him and you than him and the eagle."

"Now I'm embarrassed."

"Don't be. Just keep that in mind. And you ought to be getting back to bed. It's late, we're almost done—I can finish up with these last few."

"I'm enjoying this so much, having the chance to visit with you. What will you do about Tyler?"

"I just don't know. He's got me stumped. The magic isn't working."

"Cody says Tyler watches the bear cub a lot, through the fence. Has he ever asked if he can wear the bear suit, feed the bear?"

"No, but he would never come right out and ask. I could try that. Unless Tyler might hurt the cub, that is."

"He wouldn't," I said.

"What makes you so sure? I'd like to give him a chance, but when he's with the bear, we'd have to be able to trust him. We can't be spying on him, or it's pointless."

"When he was holding Liberty, the way he looked, I honestly don't think that was about me watching him. I think that was the *real* Tyler, when he wasn't on guard, trying to act how his father expects him to."

Jackie raised an eyebrow at me.

"I really believe it, Jackie. You know what I think? Tyler regrets what he did. He's just so locked inside himself, he can't show what he feels. He thought Liberty was wonderful. If he could be the one to feed the bear cub, all by himself. . . ."

"You just sold me. It's a huge risk, but I'll try it."

"One more thing before I go back to bed, Jackie. . . . What are Liberty's chances?"

"Not good, Shannon. She's still not standing up."

"Why do you think Neal got so attached to her? He never does that, right? With the other animals, he doesn't check back after he delivers them. He brings 'em, Jackie fixes 'em?"

"Pretty much. Once in a while he'll come into the clinic when we're having trouble handling an animal, usually a raccoon. Otherwise he stays away. He never says much about why. Neal is not a big talker about his own feelings, about personal matters, as you may have noticed. What I do know is that your uncle has more feeling for the emotions and secret lives of animals than anyone I've ever met."

"What are you getting at?"

"You know not all our animals make it. We can't save them all. I'm just guessing, but I think he can't bear to let himself care too much about them after he rescues them. He'd have his heart broken over and over. He tries to keep his mind on doing what he can. But like I said, he's not much for talking about his feelings."

"My mother told me before we left: 'Not a great communicator but as good a person as you'll ever meet.'"

"Well, here's my theory about Neal and Liberty. Something about that magnificent bird, how vulnerable she is, just pushed him over the edge. He couldn't help caring about her, and now he's hooked. Up till now he's always held something back, always tried to protect himself emotionally. With Liberty he just couldn't, so he's giving it his all."

"He'll be crushed if she doesn't pull herself together."

"I know," Jackie said softly.

I flashed on Tyler and the opposite point of view. "Jackie, what do you say to someone who says most of these animals aren't worth saving? Like all these baby squirrels, the little skunks, the baby birds?"

"A life is a life," Jackie said without hesitation. "That's what I say. A life is a life. It's not ours to decide which are worth saving and which aren't."

"I understand," I said. "Thank you for that, Jackie, and thank you for everything. My parents would kiss your feet."

She waved me away. "They might have pigeon droppings on them or worse."

On my way back to bed I checked in on Cody. He wasn't jabbering with dogs or with the wildlife this time, he was chewing on his blankie, and with a vengeance.

No doubt he was having a nightmare. Only the day before he'd shown me a photograph in his *Book of Disasters* of a softball-sized meteorite that had crashed through the roof of a house and then through the floor at the foot of a kid's bed. What disaster was he tilting with now?

11

THE DAY OF THE HAWK

I finally got to sleep, only to end up fighting a nightmare myself, an old one that was back like a disease. I was in an airplane that had been hijacked by terrorists who were flying us right at a skyscraper. A moment before the impact I saw people jump up from their desks. They were looking at us and we were looking at them. Somehow Cody and I survived the collision and found ourselves inside the building. In the dark and the smoke and amid the screams, we started racing down the stairs. After what seemed like forever—everybody kept falling on one another—we had only reached the forty-sixth floor, and time was running out. The whole building was about to come down.

Finally I got so scared, I blinked myself awake. And there was Cody, standing by my bed. "Something's different," he said. "It's all cloudy. It's starting to rain."

By now I was awake enough to see he was clutching his blankie. There was a hurt look on his face. "What is it?" I said.

"Uncle Neal got hurt."

I sat up. "How, Cody? What happened? How bad is he hurt?"

"It was in a dream, Shan."

"Oh, thank goodness. Don't scare me like that! Come, sit on the bed and tell me about it."

He sat on the bedside, sort of hiding his blankie with his leg. It used to picture Mickey Mouse from *The Sorcerer's Apprentice*, with the wand and the wizard's hat, but these days you had to fill in quite a bit with your imagination. Cody had been on the verge of retiring his blankie when September 11 happened. "Go ahead, Cody," I told him. "It's good to talk about your bad dreams."

Even though I haven't been talking about my own, I thought.

"Okay, Uncle Neal was on a steep roof trying to kill a cat with a hockey stick."

"Cody, Uncle Neal does not kill cats."

"I know, but he doesn't like how they kill so many birds, and Tyler killed a dog with a stick. It all got mixed together."

"I can see that, but how did you know what Tyler did?"

"Robbie told me. The bad part of my dream was, Uncle Neal slipped when he was trying to kill the cat and fell off the roof. He got hurt really bad. He had to go to the hospital."

I gave him a hug. "This is not a big deal, Cody. Strange things happen in dreams. I ought to know, I have my share of weird ones."

"Bad ones, scary ones?"

"Last night I had one about the World Trade Center—the airplanes and the towers. I've had it before."

Cody crumpled. "Don't talk about that, Shannie!"

"Okay," I said. "I just mentioned it to show you it's still bothering me, too. As for your dream, it just shows how much you care about Uncle Neal. Of course you don't want him to get hurt."

"Is it okay if I tell him not to go up on any roofs?"

"Maybe sometimes he needs to."

"What if I ask him not to just for today?"

"He's not going to. It's raining."

The rain kept up through the morning. It was still raining when we got on the road. "This is more like it!" Uncle Neal exclaimed as we took off. "I've got some genuine Seattle weather to show you. The beat of the wipers is music to my ears. We get nine months of this!"

"I'm sure glad we came in the summer," I said.

"The dry season is for wimps!" the Midnight Rambler declared as he swerved off the road and into a drive-through espresso. Neal waited with the window open. His sleeve was getting wet but that didn't seem to bother him.

Neal took the hot paper cup and cradled it in his hands. "Before people ever drank these, they used them for hand warmers."

"He's goofy today," Cody said from the back.

"No, I'm Pluto. I feel good, you guys." Neal took a long sip from his coffee, then set it in the cup holder. "Ahhh . . . I'm on top of the world, I'm the king of the world! Liberty snatched a herring right out of my hand this morning. With vigor. Sun, sun, go away, there's nothing like a rainy day."

"Does that mean she stood up?" I asked hopefully.

"No, but . . ."

I quickly changed the subject. "Uncle Neal, remember the first time you visited back East, before Cody was born?"

"I remember it well. You were five."

"That's right, and I remember sitting on the park bench at the end of the block with you. Dad was pointing out the famous skyscrapers: the Empire State Building, the Chrysler Building, the . . ."

I hesitated, on account of Cody, then finished my sentence anyway: " . . . the World Trade Center towers."

From the backseat, a very loud silence.

"It's okay to talk about them," I said over my shoulder. "It would be sad if we didn't remember them. Cody, you'll like this. Uncle Neal started telling us how the skyscrapers in Seattle are covered with moss, from all the rain. I remember that, trying to picture it."

"Ha! That's a good one!"

Neal found Cody in the rearview mirror. "Come back in October, Cody. That's when the rains kick in and the moss starts to grow. Why do you think people here call it the Emerald City?"

I said, "Mom told me the real reason. She said people from Seattle hype the bad weather so it won't get too crowded."

Uncle Neal laughed. "So you're on to us. Is that so bad?"

"Bumper sticker!" the kid in the backseat yelled. "Uncle Neal, get closer."

"Cody, we're going seventy," I said. "You want to tailgate, in the rain?"

Neal did edge a little closer.

"What does it say, Shannie, what does it say? Something about a toilet!"

"Cody . . ."

"I got it! POLICE STATION TOILET STOLEN—COPS HAVE NOTHING TO GO ON. That's the best of all time!"

"Write it down so you won't forget it, Cody."

"I'm writing it down now!"

Uncle Neal reached for his coffee. "The rest of the summer will be downhill from here."

"I've got one," I nearly shouted. "It applies to you, Cody. ALWAYS REMEMBER YOU'RE UNIQUE—JUST LIKE EVERYBODY ELSE."

Neal drove us to a golf course overlooking Lake Washington. Our mission was to free a hawk that was tangled in a net on the driving range. It was drizzling when we got there, but people were out on the course playing golf. "A day without sunshine is like a day in Seattle," Uncle Neal said as we parked at the pro shop.

From the parking lot we could see the bird in the net. Fortunately it wasn't very high off the ground. It had to be a large bird if we could make it out from so far away. We drove out to the hawk in style, a carrier and a folding chair fastened on the back of our golf cart with bungee cords. Sage had to stay in the ambulance.

The hawk was hanging upside down. "Must've bounced when it hit the net," Neal said. "Bounced and got its talons entangled. It doesn't look hurt, really. What a beauty, a full-grown red-tailed hawk. We should have it on its way shortly." Neal pulled the heavy welding gloves over his light buckskin gloves.

The sun was coming out, and I was distracted by a glorious rainbow over Lake Washington. I didn't really see what happened.

Uncle Neal had climbed onto the chair and was starting to go to work. It was going to be a slow process with his clumsy gloves. I heard him say, "Oh," just "Oh," like he was mildly surprised about something. I looked up and saw spatters on his sunglasses. It took me a second to realize it was blood, fresh blood. I had no idea what was going on. I guess

I thought it was from the hawk.

Supporting his left hand with his right, Neal got down off the chair, staring at his left glove. The heel of the glove's thumb had a clean slice through it, as if it was defective. Uncle Neal looked extremely confused, and then he said, "Must've got me."

Neal held up his left hand, and we both saw something new. Blood was streaming down his forearm. I stared but still couldn't make sense of it.

"It can't be that bad," Neal said. "I didn't feel a thing. Slip the welding glove off for me, will you, Shannon? Slow and easy."

I worked it off as gently as possible, only to discover that the buckskin glove underneath was completely soaked with blood. Then I saw. Neal was cut clean through the inside glove too. His thumb was laid back, laid completely open. Just like raw meat. Tendons cut, his whole thumb askew like it could fall off. I was going dizzy and had to fight turning away.

Uncle Neal's eyes went wide. "I didn't feel a thing. I didn't even know it got me."

I was so stunned, all I could say was the obvious: "This is bad, Uncle Neal."

He was still looking at his hand like it was someone else's. He said calmly, "I can't believe I lost my focus like that."

"You have a first-aid kit in the ambulance, right? Where is it?"

"The medical kit is under the back seat. We'll get some bandages."

"Let's get going, then," I said urgently. "Cody!" I yelled. He was pretty far off, kicking golf balls, soccer-style, into the net.

The hawk beat its wings, then was still again. Neal looked

up at it. The hawk blinked at him fiercely. Upside down in the net like that, who would have thought it could have been a threat?

"Not without the bird," Uncle Neal said. "If we leave the hawk, it'll die."

He shucked the welding glove off his right hand and fished a pocketknife out of his jeans. "Open it up for me, Shannon."

"Uncle Neal, forget the bird." Tears burned at my eyes.

He shook his head. "I can't just leave him. Not to mention Jackie is crazy about redtails. She'd skin me alive."

I opened the blade and handed it to him. Neal stepped onto the folding chair and started hacking at the net around the bird. "At least it didn't get my right hand."

Meanwhile Neal's left hand was hanging at his side, streaming blood.

By this time Cody was standing there, wondering what was going on. From my voice he knew that something was very wrong. He hadn't noticed Uncle Neal's left hand yet, didn't have a clue.

"You can't do that one-handed," I said. "Let me do it."

Uncle Neal got down off the chair, handed me the knife, cradled his left hand with his right. Then Cody saw. He went pale and looked away.

"Just don't come near those talons," Uncle Neal warned me.

"Don't worry, I won't." The knife was sharp, thank goodness. I cut a wide circle around the bird.

"His left foot isn't tangled at all," Neal said with sudden understanding. "I just assumed it was. He's holding himself with that left foot, and the back talon is free. Look, Cody, that back talon is what got me."

I don't know if Cody looked. I sure didn't. I was keeping

my eyes on what I was doing and working as fast as possible without cutting my fingers off.

"Will they get mad about their net?" Cody wondered.

Through gritted teeth, Neal said, "They can patch it back together."

With a quick glance at his face I saw the pain had kicked in, extreme pain. "We have to save this bird," Neal said, "or this is all for nothing."

The more net I cut loose, the more the bird got tangled. I had to keep one eye on its talons so I didn't get anywhere close to them. "Get the carrier ready, Cody."

Eyes big as saucers, Cody jumped into action.

"There," I said, holding the tangle of net with the hawk inside as I cut the last strand. I stepped down with the bird and eased it through the carrier door. "Let's get you to the hospital," I said to Neal.

"University Medical Center," he said. "It's not far away. Great job with the bird, Shannon."

We boarded the cart and drove straight to the door of the van. Cody threw the door open and whipped out the medical kit. I managed to remove the buckskin glove from Uncle Neal's injured left hand without pulling off his thumb, which was a minor miracle.

His hand was a gruesome sight. I wrapped it around and around with gauze bandaging, firm enough to slow the bleeding. I stowed the carrier in the back and then we were out of there.

"Drive carefully," I told Uncle Neal. "I'm sure you're in shock. Cody, is your seatbelt fastened?"

"Got it."

I said to Neal, "You've been feeling it awhile now."

"Oh yeah, I can feel it."

At the emergency room, they told Uncle Neal he was in

luck. The best surgeon in Seattle for what he needed was here in the hospital and not operating at the moment. They'd send for her right away.

"I'll call Jackie," I told Uncle Neal. "She'll take care of everything."

"That she will. You guys take care of Sage, Jackie will take care of the hawk."

Uncle Neal was led away to an examining room. I called the center and got Rosie. Jackie was away releasing animals, but Rosie was going to come as soon as she could. She would bring another driver for the van. As I hung up I realized that Neal hadn't given me the keys.

I got Cody settled in the waiting area off of the emergency room. All of a sudden he got this intense look as he reached for a magazine. On the cover was an erupting volcano.

I told the emergency room receptionist my problem. She said she'd get the van keys for me. I asked if I could go myself and tell Neal what they said at the wildlife center. "First room on the right," she said. "He's still waiting for the doctor."

I hesitated as I approached. There were voices from inside the room, Neal's and a woman's. The doctor was already there. I sat down on the chair outside and waited.

"No medications since the first of June? Where do you stand with your treatments?"

"I'm in a wait-and-see. I have an appointment for the twenty-fifth of August—that'll be thirteen months after I got the diagnosis."

"How did you handle the chemotherapy?"

"I was up and down with it. I just hope it's all behind me."

Chemotherapy. The word hit me so hard I couldn't breathe.

Chemotherapy. Doesn't that mean cancer?

Of course. Of course. It was all starting to make sense. The chemicals in the medicines make your hair fall out. That's why he started shaving his head.

Chemotherapy. That's what made him so thin, so weak.

"You have damage to tendons and nerves," the doctor was saying. "That hawk missed the artery feeding your hand, just barely. We can be thankful for that. I'm going to have to put you under, and it's going to be a lengthy operation. No allergies to any anesthesia we might use?"

"Just one question." Uncle Neal joked. "Who's going to end up with my thumb, you or me?"

I got up quietly. I'd tell the receptionist I couldn't find him. She'd bring me the keys.

Cancer. Of course. No wonder he doesn't look the same, no wonder he had to give up climbing, no wonder!

Uncle Neal, Uncle Neal . . . Why didn't you tell us?

12

LIFE CAN BE LIKE THAT

It was terrible leaving the hospital without Uncle Neal, but the surgery was going to be long and hard and complicated. After he was out of surgery it was going to take him a while to come out of the anesthesia.

As we started back to the center, Rosie handed me her cell phone and told me to call Jackie, who was on her way back from releasing a spotted owl in the Cascade Mountains. As calmly as I could, I told her what had happened to Uncle Neal. I told her that the hawk was in the van, which was right behind us on the freeway. "Neal wouldn't leave the hawk behind," I said, "even after it hurt him so bad."

"That's Neal," Jackie replied, her voice cracking.

"Actually, he said you'd skin him alive if he left it."

"That's Neal too. He went up on a slippery roof during a lightning storm once and came down with a redtail. Your uncle claimed I would have wrung his neck if he didn't

rescue it. I just hope everything goes well with his operation. You guys hurry home."

Rosie's car was awful quiet as she drove north. It was
tight with the three of us squeezed in the front, but the
closeness felt good. Cody said, "If Dad wasn't in Pakistan he
could fix Uncle Neal up. "

"That's right," I said. "Dad does that kind of surgery."

"But he's in Pakistan."

I hugged my brother. "That's right, Cody. Peshawar,
Pakistan. With Mom, doing fine. Helping all those families
who live in tents."

"I'm still mad at that hawk."

"I know you are. But think how scared the hawk was,
hanging upside down in that net. It's such a wild thing, and
it was afraid. Not that I'm not mad at it too."

Rosie gave Cody a pat on the knee. "They'll fix your uncle
up just fine."

I thought, I'm even madder at Uncle Neal for not telling
his family he had cancer. First chance I get when it's just the
two of us, I'm going to let him have it.

I wanted to talk to Rosie about what she knew about the
cancer, what Jackie knew, but not in front of Cody. Now I
knew what Jackie had been getting at, that first morning at
the center. We were talking about Neal, things my mother
didn't know about him. Jackie had looked at me funny and
said, "Anything else she doesn't know?"

That's exactly when Jackie figured out that Neal still
hadn't told us.

Now I knew why Jackie flinched as we were feeding the
baby squirrels, when I asked if Neal had been making night
runs with the ambulance even before he was laid off by
Boeing. Had he actually been laid off?

It was all coming together, finally. Duh, it had taken me

long enough to figure it out. Boeing started laying workers off soon after the attacks of September 11, when lots of people suddenly stopped flying. The demand for new airplanes was taking a nosedive. After September 11, that's when my mother thought her brother had quit working, but it must have been a month or so before. Neal would have left his job to start the chemotherapy treatments, which were going to make him sick. He was already on medical leave when the World Trade Center and the Pentagon were attacked.

And he hadn't told his sister. That's the part that really got me. He didn't want her to know he had cancer. When Boeing started laying people off, he let his sister think he was unemployed, not sick.

My uncle had told me he wasn't such a great communicator. Well, that was the understatement of the year.

Time dragged. At last we got off the interstate. I wanted to talk with Jackie so bad. Finally Cedar Glen came in sight, and at last the JACKIE'S WILD SEATTLE sign. Did everybody at the center but Cody and me know? What kind of cancer was it? One of the really awful kinds?

At last we were back. There was Jackie, waiting in front of the office. We jumped out of Rosie's car and flew toward her. "I just talked to the hospital," Jackie said. "Neal is still in surgery. We can see him tomorrow morning."

Jackie's eyes went to the wildlife ambulance pulling in behind us. "I better take care of the hawk," she said. She kissed each of us on the cheek.

Cody was about to cry. "I'm gonna see Chuckie," he said, and ran into the clinic.

I grabbed Jackie by the arm. "I need to talk. As soon as you can."

She saw how intense I was. "Where will you be?"

"In your office. I'm going to check my e-mail."

I jumped on the computer. Whether or not I'd heard from my parents, I had news to report to them. Uncle Neal news. I'd start with what the hawk did to his thumb, then I'd tell them about the cancer.

I caught myself. It was okay to tell them about the hawk, but the second item, that would be a bombshell, especially for my mother. And I still knew next to nothing, not even what kind of cancer it was.

I typed in my password. I had mail.

It didn't mean I was finally hearing from my parents. I'd been getting e-mails from my friends in Weehawken right along.

This time, I found one from Lisa, one from Rebecca, one from Matt, and then, almost too good to be true, there they were: one-two-three from my parents.

I scanned them as fast as I could to find out if anything was wrong. As far as I could make out, there wasn't. I went back and read every word. The first message, from my mother, said they were fine. Everything was okay. They'd just heard from Doctors Without Borders that we hadn't been getting their messages. They were so sorry. Their palm device had been receiving our messages just fine. One of the doctors being rotated out would send these new ones from Islamabad.

The second message, from my father, told where they actually were:

Our camp in the Pakistani desert near Peshawar is called New Jalozai. We can only guess at its population, still tens of thousands. Every day more families leave for Afghanistan even though there is little to go back to after twenty-four years of war, and the drought hangs on. Next door to us is Old Jalozai with well over a hundred thousand last winter. Your mother and I are in the midst of the greatest refugee crisis in the world—more than a million victims.

I am performing operations in the clinic (such as it is) night and day. As I stumbled back to our tent to sleep this morning I came upon a boy flying a kite above the open sewer that runs through the camp. He smiled at me. There was still a child inside him, still hope, and that was wonderful to see. I have never felt better about being a doctor. Thank you, Shannon, thank you, Cody, for your love and support. Jackie's center sounds fantastic. Have a happy summer with Uncle Neal rescuing the animals. We think of you all the time, we miss you, and we love you. Dad.

I was already bawling before I started my mom's next message:

Cody, don't worry about our safety. You too, Shannon. People in the camp are so kind. What they went through to get here is nearly beyond belief. In the remote areas of Afghanistan, many died last winter—from cold, disease, and starvation. The food from the relief agencies never got to some of them. They mixed grass with the little flour they had in order to make bread for their children. For years, one out of every four children has been dying before the age of five. The smiles of the kids would break your heart. I am vaccinating against measles and polio, seeing to the women who have been neglected for so long.

We're proud that you are helping your uncle and the wildlife center this summer. You are helping to heal the world. Each of us can only make a small difference but together we can make a big difference. I'm so happy you have this chance to spend "quality time" with Uncle Neal. Be brave, Cody. That little beaver sounds so cool, and good luck with Sage. Don't fret, Shannon, all will be well, I promise. Enjoy your summer, take care of each other. With hugs, love, and kisses to all three of you, Mom.

The door opened. It was Jackie. Her eyes were wide, seeing me so emotional. "I finally heard from my parents," I sobbed. "They're fine, everything's fine."

I stood up and went to her. She held me and I just kept sobbing.

Jackie stroked my hair and held me close. She said, "I just can't tell you how happy that makes me to hear that."

I recovered enough to stand back and wipe my eyes. I reached for the tissues on her desk.

"I'm so relieved," I said. "I'm just so relieved."

"Do you want to run and get Cody and tell him the news?"

"Not yet," I said. "First, can we talk about Uncle Neal? Did you know about him having cancer?"

Jackie was taken aback. "So you know. . . . Yes, I've known it almost a year. Did Tyler tell you?"

I shook my head. "Why did you say that?"

"Well, he knows. I've been half-expecting he'd tell you, or tell Cody."

"He didn't. I overheard Neal and the doctor talking in the emergency room. But I don't know any more about it. Tell me everything you know."

"All right, I'll do my best." Jackie ran her hand through

her gray hair. She looked old and worn-out. "Neal had been real tired for months, but kept thinking it was just the hours he was working full time at Boeing and weekends here. Then he discovered a lump under his arm, a swelling that didn't go away. When he finally went to the doctor about it, they did some tests and said he had lymphoma, which is cancer of the lymphatic system. They took out some lymph nodes and gave him radiation at the site. Then he had a long course of chemotherapy to attack it wherever it might be spreading through his body. I'm so sorry about this, Shannon. It must be such a terrible shock for you."

"I just really wish I had known. My mother doesn't even know. Do you realize that?"

Jackie heaved a sigh and nodded.

"I mean, he didn't even tell his sister. Why? Why wouldn't he?"

"Neal hates like the dickens the idea of anybody feeling sorry for him. We both know he isn't so good at sharing his feelings. My guess is he didn't want to tell his sister, didn't want to worry her, until he knew he had the battle won, or knew he'd lost it, for that matter."

"Then why do people at the center know?"

"We were going to be seeing him every day. With all his doctor's appointments, and the times he'd be sick from the treatments, well, he had to level with us. But he let it be known he didn't want to have to talk about being sick. He's very big on positive thinking, trying only to think about being well."

I stood there shaking my head. "I can just picture how he got into this situation with me and Cody coming out even though he was sick. When my mother called him a few weeks before school got out, she was all fired up to answer

the call from Doctors Without Borders. Actually, I heard her
end of the conversation. She didn't realize I was listening,
but I was. She called up Neal all excited for him to say yes.
What choice did he have?"

Jackie touched me on the shoulder. "It wasn't only to help
out his sister, Shannon. He wanted the time with you and
Cody."

Time, I thought. Time was the key word, how much of it
Uncle Neal might have. This summer, these nine weeks,
could be the last time he'd ever see us. I swallowed hard and
asked, "How bad is lymphoma?"

"It can be deadly, but it also can be survivable. If it's
gonna get you, it usually takes a few years and sometimes a
lot more. It's possible to beat it completely, walk away
cancer-free."

Fiercely, I said, "Then that's the way it's going to be."

"I believe that too. He'll find out shortly after you guys
are back home if it's still in his body. Then he'll take it from
there. Having you guys here . . . maybe he was anxious at
first about how it would work out, but haven't you noticed
what it's done for him? He's crazy about you two. I've
known Neal for years, and never seen him happier."

I started sniffling. "You should have seen him in the van
this morning, all hyper, before he got hurt. I just don't know
how I feel. I feel too many things at once. A few minutes ago
I was so sure I was going to tell him I was mad at him for
not telling us."

"But now you're looking at it from his point of view. If he
had told you, what would the summer have been like for you
and Cody, for all three of you?"

"So what do I do? Part of me really wants to tell my parents, but I'm already worrying what that will do to them.

Will my mother think she has to come home?"

"Could happen," Jackie said. "It's not an easy decision. You have a lot to think about. It's your call, Shannon."

"If I tell Uncle Neal I know, everything will be so different. How will he be able to keep it fun with us, stay positive, concentrate on beating the cancer? What about Cody when he finds out? Cody's going to take it real hard. Nothing will be the same."

"You don't have to decide right away, or even before you see him at the hospital. This is complicated. Life can be like that. Sometimes it's hard to know the right thing to do, no matter how hard you try. You do your best. Just remember what it's like for your uncle. He has his weaknesses, but he has amazing strengths."

That's all it took; I started sobbing again. When I got myself together, I said, "At least I understand a few things I didn't before. I understand why you wanted Uncle Neal to move up here with you. It was so you could look after him."

"The only reason it worked out was because he needed more space for you and Cody."

"I understand more about him and Liberty, too. That's about *both* of them getting well, isn't it?"

"You're a sharp one, Shannon."

"I'm dense! I mean, there isn't a hair on his head, and I'm like, 'Duh!' "

I started laughing. Laughing-crying. "How *is* Liberty?"

"No better. Sooner or later we're going to have to release her to the eagle spirit world."

"You mean put her down."

"Put her down. If she doesn't want to live, well, Neal knows it's a matter of weeks, not months. On a happier note, he'll be pleased to hear that the red-tailed hawk you guys saved today is in perfect condition. She lost two flight feathers but that's no big deal. Cody told me how you cut her loose, and how careful you were with her. We're just about to release her. Come and see."

Outside, everybody was assembling for the release. Rosie was there and so were a dozen or so volunteers, including Tyler in the bear suit. He was holding the head piece in his hand. I was kind of surprised that he let himself be rounded up for the event. Cody was there, peering into the carrier.

Jackie told everybody the short version of what had happened at the driving range. She said that the doctor who operated on Uncle Neal's hand told her there was a good chance he'd get full use of it back. Then she said that Cody and I had showed "courage under fire."

Cody opened the carrier door. The big hawk came out slowly, glared at everybody standing there, then took to the sky accompanied by cheers, lots and lots of cheers.

13

DOES IT HURT?

At least for this morning it's all about his hand, just his hand. That's what I told myself on our way up to Uncle Neal's hospital room. No looking deep into his soul. If in doubt, keep it light.

Uncle Neal's hand was in a soft cast that was wrapped in gauze from his knuckles to the middle of his forearm. "Does it. hurt?" Cody asked.

"Only when I laugh at how dumb I was," Neal said. "I took an IQ test and the results were negative."

"Wait a second," I said. "That sounds suspiciously like a bumper sticker."

"It is," he confessed. "Nothing is foolproof for a sufficiently talented fool."

"Wait another second," Cody said. "That sounds like a bumper sticker too."

"IIow about this one?" Jackie chimed in. "The two most common elements in the universe are hydrogen and stupidity."

"This is sickening," Cody said. "Everyone in this whole room likes bumper stickers."

Everyone was laughing. That was when I made my decision. As much as I hated to, I was going to keep Uncle Neal's secret. We had too much to lose, all the way around.

Neal came home later that day. He wasn't going to be able to use his left hand for a couple of weeks. Using it fully, that was going to take months. Forget about rescuing animals, I thought, but I didn't say it.

When Neal got back to the center he went straight to Liberty. He spent hour upon hour sitting with her. With his hurt hand on his lap he would stroke her chest feathers with his fingertips and talk, talk, talk with her.

For a while at least, no midnight rambles for him. I looked in on him three nights in a row. My uncle must have been exhausted; the first two nights I found him sound asleep. The third night he caught me. A light was on and he was reading. "Anything wrong, Shannon? Can't sleep?"

I stepped inside and sat in his rocking chair. Sage got up from the throw rug alongside Neal's bed, lay down next to me, and let me pet the crown of her head. "Cody would be so jealous," I said. Then, after a pause, "How are you doing? Healing?"

"I sure think so."

"Good. Are you bummed that you can't be rescuing animals in the middle of the night?"

He looked surprised. "I thought I was being so careful not to wake you."

My eyebrows went up disapprovingly.

"It wasn't every night. I just don't sleep much."

"You slept the last couple of nights. It shows it can be done."

"They put me so far under at the hospital, it took me a couple days to get my normal metabolism back." With a grin, he added, "Hey, I'm a restless soul."

"Too much coffee if you ask me."

"I should have told you about my night runs, Shannon. Didn't want you to worry. I have some peculiar ways."

"I've noticed that."

"You might have noticed I don't have a lot of close friends. I'm not so great on my people skills."

"I wouldn't say that, except with Tyler, I suppose."

"To tell you the truth, I get along with animals better than I do with most people. They're a lot more honest, a lot more straightforward, a lot more dignified. I'm a strange one— your mother should have told you."

"It's hard to figure out what to tell people and what not to," I said.

"I actually envy the animals sometimes. Instinct is so strong with them. A deer knows how to be a deer, a raven knows how to be a raven. Every single one of us has to struggle to find out what it means to be human. We are so capable of messing up it's not funny. Sometimes it's hard to keep your sense of humor. You know what I mean?"

Around his eyes, he looked so sad. I said, "Can't you just clap your hands together real loud and frighten Liberty into standing up?"

"Tried it," he said with a strangled laugh. "Liberty's on your mind too?"

"A lot, especially because you care about her so much."

"I've been trying to give her my life force. She hears me. Oh, she hears me. I haven't given up on her by a long shot. That girl's going to make it, I know she will."

* * *

Time slowed down once we were no longer chasing around in the rescue van. I learned to milk the goats, helped out in Jackie's garden some, and assisted at the clinic. I got to know lots of the volunteers by name, picked blackberries by the gallon, made some jams and pies in Jackie's kitchen.

Sometimes I would accompany Cody to the creek that ran through the valley. It was about a ten-minute walk. At the creek it was shady and cool, a great place to hang out. I would read while he tried to catch frogs. They weren't that easy to grab. The third time we went, Cody told me this was the same creek where Tyler killed the dog. I asked him how he knew that, and he said that it was somebody at Robbie's school who saw it happen.

At Jackie's these days, there was a deer hanging around the garden fence, browsing, twitching her tail and keeping her large ears attuned to the golden retrievers. Once in a while the dogs hassled her, but generally they were oblivious on the office porch. The deer was biding her time, Jackie said, waiting for us to leave the garden gate open.

The doe was bigger than our deer in the East. Jackie said it was a mule deer, named after the big ears. Jackie was pretty sure the doe was pregnant. Midsummer was late for dropping a fawn but sometimes the animals got off schedule. The year before, the center took care of a baby rock dove that hatched in November.

One day Cody and I followed the deer through the trees and around the edge of Jackie's five acres. At the deer pen she visited the crippled doe whose job was to keep orphaned fawns company. The two touched noses through the chain-link fence.

One of those slow days, as I was heading with my novel for some shady quiet time in Jackie's cedar grove, a voice from behind me called my name. It was Tyler, just getting off work.

I let him catch up. "What's up?" I asked.

He shrugged, caught my eye, then looked away. "I don't know, just wondered if you wanted to hang out. You know, just talk. You want to take a walk or something?"

I didn't think so—I'd been staying away—but I didn't say so. "I have to stay within shouting distance of Cody. He's over there with Robbie. Over here in the trees there's a nice cool spot."

"Perfect."

I climbed up onto my stump and Tyler followed. I sat down cross-legged and he did the same. "Sweet," he said.

"It's the perfect spot. I can see the door to Jackie's house and the door to the clinic. I can hang in the shade but stay tuned to everybody's comings and goings."

"You like it here, don't you?"

"Oh yeah, I like the people, I like the animals, I like everything about it."

Tyler didn't say anything, he just scraped a little swath clear of cedar needles. But then he said, "It's kind of growing on me, too. I couldn't stand it for a long time—I've been coming here since school got out. But now I kind of look forward to it."

It can't be because we've been seeing each other lately, I thought, because we haven't. "What made the difference?" I asked him.

He closed his fist on a little pile of needles, lifted his hand, and started sifting them out the bottom, sprinkling a line across the patch he'd cleared. "To tell you the truth, I kind of expected everything to go south, but it never has." He laughed. "People don't get mad around here. I mean, even like Jackie. She's pretty serious—everything has to be done just so—but she never gets angry, really. Your uncle— I can tell he doesn't like me, but at least he doesn't go out of his way to tell me about it. That's kind of refreshing."

Tyler needed to talk. Did I really want to go there, wherever this was headed? Yet if I didn't, who would?

Why was it I had never believed he was a hopeless case? In a flash, I could picture him at the creek, what he'd done, and I pictured his father's face in the driveway.

I took a leap of faith. "At home," I began, "I guess it's not so easy?"

"You got that right. It's never been easy. My old man's got a temper like you wouldn't believe."

"I'm sorry. Cody and I are lucky in the parent department."

"I heard about your parents going to Pakistan and all that. That whole part of the world is dangerous, isn't it?"

"It's definitely something to worry about."

"Both doctors, that's pretty impressive. I'm the son of a mechanic and a checker at Wal-Mart."

"So, how come you're putting that down? What's wrong with either of those?"

He looked at me skeptically.

"My parents weren't *born* doctors," I said. "My dad's parents were farmers. My mother was the daughter of a warehouse manager and a clerk at the Department of Motor Vehicles. This is America, Tyler."

He glanced at me like I'd made a speech, which I guess I had. "I know, I know. What I should have said was, sometimes I wish my father would go to Pakistan for a nice long vacation."

"Really?"

He laughed and said, "Sure. It would be a break for me and my mom."

To that, I didn't know what to say. I wanted to run away from the topic but I got brave and said, "I guess you don't mind getting out of the house to come to the center, even if it's not by choice. It gets you away from your dad."

"Right. This is all working out pretty good this summer. I can't drive yet so I can't get very far away, but this place kind of gives me a place to hide out. I just wish it made more sense."

"How do you mean?"

"Don't get me wrong, but what happened to 'survival of the fittest' and all that? I mean, rehabbing birds and squirrels that cats have dragged in, and raccoons that have been hit by cars. What happened to letting nature take its course?"

I didn't even have to think about it. I'd been thinking about it since he started talking like this the last time. "Tyler, there isn't any 'nature' anymore."

"No nature?"

"I mean, we've interfered too much. We keep taking away land from them and using it for ourselves. Isn't it true what Jackie says, how every year there's more people, more cars and roads and buildings, and less room for wildlife? What's natural about cars hitting the animals, people's pets catching them, a hawk flying into the net at the driving range?"

"Heard about that. I'm sorry. It just seems so, well, *extreme* to try to save all these animals, like Jackie and your uncle and all these volunteers are doing. I mean, the whole earth is going to be a parking lot eventually, don't you think?"

"Maybe not. What a nightmare, Tyler. We can't give up that easy."

"I'm just coming from such a different place. I started talking to my dad about the bear cub, me dressing up in the suit and all—it made him so crazy. I wanted to tell him that with certain animals at least, what the center does makes a lot of sense, actually. Like with the birds of prey, the bear cub, definitely the bear cub."

"Well, tell me about that. I haven't heard about the cub. Tell me what it's like."

"You really want to know?"

"Hey, I'm jealous. You've been getting closer to it than anybody."

Tyler was suddenly all lit up. "It's amazing to be wearing that bear suit, and to be that close. He only used to eat mush that was a mixture of fruit, fish, dog chow, and a bunch of other stuff. He still gets that, but I also bring him blackberry branches and logs that I fill with mealworms. He's starting to find his own food, to work for it. It's very cool, actually. And I get to play with him for like five minutes. He's all over me. I keep hoping another cub comes to the center. That's what he really needs. He has way too much energy to be alone."

"Will they actually be able to release him? Can he go completely wild and not become one of those garbage bears that raid campgrounds and stuff?"

Tyler's eyes got intense. "That's the whole idea! In January, they're going to take him up to the Cascades, to an old bear den in the snow country, and they're going to put him in it. You know, when he's tranquilized. When he wakes up and comes outside, it'll be all cold and covered with snow. He'll turn around, go back into the den, and go to sleep. In the spring, everything that happened here at Jackie's is going to seem like a dream."

"That's fantastic to think about. It really works?"

"It really works. A vet who came and shot him with a tranquilizer gun told me all about it. I got to hold the bear while the vet gave him an injection, some kind of meds once a month for parasites. I asked how the bear will find a den or know how to dig a new one the next winter, and he said instinct will take care of that."

"Amazing."

"The vet said I could go along in January when they release him. I told him I'd be in school. He said no problem, we'll figure it out. I doubt if my dad would let me, though. If it didn't have anything to do with Jackie, maybe he would, but as it is—"

Suddenly Tyler looked at his watch. His face went pale. "Gotta jet. I was supposed to be home ten minutes ago."

He started to climb down off the stump. "Tyler," I said.

He looked back up. I said, "Well, just take it easy."

"Sure," he said. "You too, Shannon."

14

TURTLES FOR PEACE

When Neal wasn't with Liberty, he was more restless than the caged animals. He was used to roaming all of Pierce, King, and Snohomish counties. I understood. If he slowed down he'd start thinking about the cancer. He'd give anything to be on the road again and rescuing the animals.

And I had a solution. I'd been thinking it over and over. Our eighth day grounded at the center, I began by asking Neal about how he was doing. "It's killing me that I can't be out doing the hot rescues," he admitted.

"I thought so," I said. "I miss it too. And Jackie's having to turn down a lot of calls. We don't want the police departments and sheriffs' departments and all the other people to quit calling."

"Exactly my thoughts, Shannon, but what can we do about it?"

"Well, you can still *drive*. You've been driving Jackie's station wagon into Cedar Glen to the espresso place."

"Yeah, it's an automatic. No problem."

"Well, so is the ambulance. You could drive the ambulance."

"Sure, I could still drive. It's catching the critters one-handed that's the problem."

I held up both of mine. "Here are your catchers, Uncle Neal. You coach, I catch."

It took another minute for him to take me seriously. Then he took me really seriously. He allowed that I was fast enough, coordinated enough, decisive enough to do the catching. He even thought Sage would work with me. Then he backed off and talked about the danger element. "I won't grab any hawks by the talons," I promised. "Look, most of the stuff you do is a lot less dangerous than driving on the highway. We can get the team back together. You, me, Cody, and Sage."

"I'm sold," he said. "When do we start?"

"Why not tomorrow?"

The team was back together and rolling again. We were headed across Lake Washington, and it was just like old times. "The greatest thing about this job," Uncle Neal said cheerfully, "is that it's not a job."

"What's the second greatest thing?" sang the kid from the backseat as he reached out to pet Sage, hopeful she had changed her policy. She hadn't.

"It's that you never know what to expect."

I threw in, "What's the third greatest thing?"

"The bumper stickers you meet. Keep your eye out."

"What's the mission? I mean, our first mission."

"Something got into somebody's house over near Lake Sammamish. The woman didn't speak much English. I don't think she knows *what* it is."

The address led us to a new housing development. A dignified but distraught Japanese woman answered the door. She was hanging on to a huge German shepherd. The house was built on three levels into the hillside above a creek. They led us around the back of the house to a sliding glass door that was ajar. She opened it wide, pointed, and wailed. There was a trail of mud leading across the plush white carpet.

"It'll be easy to track," Cody said.

The mud trail had tracks on either side of a continuous swath. Missing the obvious, I asked, "What in the world are we after?"

"A big Chuckie!" Cody cried. "You can see where it dragged its tail!"

I raced to the van for gloves and a carrier. When I got back, Neal and Cody were taking off their shoes. I did the same. Cody was studying the trail of mud, slime, and beaver tracks leading down the hallway. The house was brand-new, yet traditionally Japanese. "Beautiful home," I said to the lady.

"No more beautiful," she said sorrowfully.

A hallway opened into the living room, and there we got the picture. It looked like a bomb had gone off: lacquered end tables knocked over, porcelain broken, lamps on the floor, chairs on their back, the luxurious white carpet slimed everywhere you looked, objets d'art scattered everywhere.

"A beaver on steroids?" I wondered.

The German shepherd was in the kitchen wagging his tail and barking his head off.

"I think the beaver had help," Uncle Neal said with a wry

lift of his eyebrows. He had the lady confine her canine in the laundry room so the dog and the beaver, wherever it was, didn't mix it up again.

We followed the trail down to the second level of the house, where the devastation was equally complete. The lady stayed behind on the stairs wringing her hands. She was terrified to go any farther.

"Strange there's no blood on the carpet," Uncle Neal said. "I don't get it."

We looked in the family room and the bedrooms. What a mess. We looked under the beds, in the closets. No beaver.

"We need Sage," I said, and Neal agreed. We trooped back to the van where I found her leash, buckled on her flak jacket and cinched it snug, then got my light gloves, my new welding gloves, and the carrier. Cody grabbed the salmon net. Neal whispered the code word in my ear. On the way down the stairs to the second level, Sage was already onto the scent before I ever cried "Slaptail!" and let her off the leash.

Sage took off like a shot, down the hallway and into the bedrooms where we'd already been, then back out through the family room and down into the third level.

By the time we caught up, Sage had come to standstill in front of a couch. She was at full alert. Everything in the basement rooms that could have been toppled, had been. "I get it," Uncle Neal said. "No wonder no blood. Her dog and the beaver were playing."

We got down on our hands and knees to peek under the couch. "Watch you don't bump Uncle Neal's cast," I cautioned Cody.

"Gotcha," he said, and gasped, "It's a Chuckie, all right. A humongous Chuckie."

Neal leaned on an elbow, craned his neck. "Biggest beaver I've seen in my life. Might go fifty pounds."

Neal had me open the door to the carrier and set it under the table next to the couch. Then I got down on my belly with the salmon net and gave the beaver a push in the table's direction. The beaver started moving, and I kept pushing. At last I shoved it out from under the couch.

By the time I scrambled to my feet to see where the beaver had gone, it had found the open carrier and crawled in. Cody closed the door and that was that.

"The carrier looked like the safest place," Neal said. "For an animal looking for cover, it often does. Not bad for our first rescue since our week off. My assistants need very little assistance. I drive, you catch."

Our next mission was to release the beaver in a place where a housing development wasn't going to put it out of business. Uncle Neal drove into the forest past a town called Issaquah. There was a stream along the road, and the houses were few and far between. He picked one that he liked and turned into the driveway across a bridge over the creek. The long drive, a riot of friendly color, was banked with tall blooming dahlias. I caught sight of a fenced vegetable garden. Out past a barn, sheep were grazing picturesquely.

As we drove up to the house, a gray-haired couple came onto the porch. Uncle Neal started by telling them he'd noticed some indications, not many, of beaver a few miles down the creek. A minute later I was opening the back of the van so they could take a look at the refugee from suburbia. Yes, they'd love to have "Big Mama Chuckie" for a neighbor. They hoped she'd stick around, find a mate, and start making ponds and some more beavers. But they wouldn't let us release her until we had lunch with them.

Her eyes on the lettering across the side of our van, the woman said her name was Jackie too, only it was spelled J-a-c-q-u-e. Her husband's name was Tom. Cody and I were checking out the bumper sticker on the back of their old pickup. It said TURTLES FOR PEACE.

As we were eating lunch on their back deck, we watched Tom and Jacque's shaggy sheepdog play a game with some crows. The dog would hide in the bushes until half a dozen crows had their crops stuffed with food from the dog dish on the lawn. Then the sheepdog would charge out of the bushes and give them a scare, which they were perfectly well expecting.

We were done with sandwiches and starting on cookies and ice cream when Cody shouted, "Will you look at that!" and took off running.

The rest of us followed. From the bushes on the far side of the backyard, a turtle was crawling into the sun. This wasn't just any turtle. It was some sort of reptilian tank.

"What in the world?" Neal said. "That's a desert tortoise."

"Well," Tom said sheepishly, "I've had that fellow for close to thirty years. I picked him up in California outside of Barstow. They've become an endangered species now, and I feel bad about taking him out of the desert. I didn't know any better at the time."

Tom asked Neal if he would see that the tortoise got taken back to the desert or at least to a zoo. Neal said Jackie had a million connections and would get it figured out.

We were about to leave, all standing around the tortoise, when the crows flew back in force, maybe a hundred darkening the sky. Strangely, one of them was white. Their raucous calls and the ominous beating of their wings had me wondering if something was about to happen.

My eyes and everyone's were drawn to the white crow. As the rest of the birds wheeled away, the white crow dropped a small object on the grass only inches from the tortoise.

The object was alive, no bigger than a fifty-cent piece, and it was a turtle. Neal picked it up and put it on his palm. "Holy cow, it's a hatchling snapping turtle. I've been trying to figure out how snapping turtles have been moving up from Oregon. Maybe it's by air."

"I'll be darned," Tom said. "Crazy crows, what a stunt."

"Those crafty corvids," Neal said, shaking his head. "Crows and ravens, you never know what to expect from them. 'You like turtles, well, here's another one for you!'"

On our way out the driveway we released the beaver and the tiny turtle into the creek. The crows were right above us, supervising, making a racket. Cody asked Neal, "Are crows and ravens really as smart as you said?"

"Sure, it's just not the kind of smartness we give credit for. That's true of animals in general. Sage's sense of smell is fifty times better than ours. We've lost most of our animal intelligence."

We made the rounds of the vets on our way back, collecting birds and squirrels and cottontail rabbits. We went to a house above Lincoln Park where a couple had evacuated on account of a bat. The bat was in the hall closet, they said. The man was clutching a tennis racket. There was stark terror in their faces.

"Not a problem," Uncle Neal told them. He had Cody find a tiny cricket cage in the jumble in the back of the ambulance. Cody returned with the cricket cage and some exciting news. Tom and Jacque, the people who had fed us lunch and given us the desert tortoise, had slapped a TURTLES FOR

PEACE bumper sticker on the back of the ambulance.

The couple followed us into the house. The man still had a death grip on his tennis racket. They pointed out the closet. Neal eased the door open; the bat was hanging on a beige overcoat. I pulled on a pair of light cotton gloves, picked the bat gently off the overcoat just like Neal told me, and put it in the cricket cage. That was it. Not exactly a big deal, but we were heroes anyhow, or so the lady said as she wrote us a check as we were leaving. I hadn't even thought to give her a donation card. We were miles away when I took the check out of my pocket. It was for ten dollars, which was pretty typical. I did a double take. She'd made it out to Turtles for Peace.

On our way home the beeper had us heading to a construction site in Snohomish to save a drowning bird. The police said they hadn't been able to get much of an explanation. It made no sense that a drowning bird could still be alive by the time we got there. We went anyway.

The address was in a new subdivision. In fact, the house we were after was just being framed up. The construction crew was taking a break as we drove in. There wasn't a stream or pond in sight, not even a bucket for a bird to drown in. The men all had silly smiles on their faces. I got out and said, "We got a call about a drowning bird. Could this be the right place?"

A guy with a walrus mustache pointed across the cul-de-sac. "In there," he said with a smirk.

He seemed to be pointing at a porta-potty. I said, "Do you mean where I think you mean?"

"Yep," he said. "That's the situation."

I went back to the ambulance and explained "the situation."

"Ugly," Neal said.

Cody pumped his fist. "This is major!"

"Since you think so," I told him, "you're on for this one. Go for it."

And he did. Neal had a box of disposable latex gloves that came in handy for the delicate operation.

The victim, a baby owl, was still alive. Cody proudly presented it to me. I took a step back. We rinsed it off with a hose at the construction site and dried it using the heater vent in the ambulance. We improvised a nest of rumpled towels in a small carrier. The baby owl burrowed into it.

The guys at the construction site were pulling out their billfolds. Most gave us tens, one gave us a twenty. One started writing a check. "Don't make it out to Turtles for Peace," Cody told him. "That's just our nickname."

"Another day at the office," Neal said as we drove out. "Life is beautiful."

This from Neal, even though he knew Liberty now had only four more days to make it. The date had been set.

I glanced across the front of the van to Uncle Neal's arms, then to his face. It looked like he'd gained a little weight since we'd come. He was still shaving his head in case he had to start the treatments again. He wouldn't miss his hair if he didn't have any.

I thought about the kid from Afghanistan flying his kite above the sewage ditch at the refugee camp, about the smile on his face.

A smile came to mine.

15

TO THE EDGE

I woke before sunrise. This was it. For three days running, Neal had stayed at Liberty's side, talking her ear off to no avail. Now the day had come. Liberty was going to have to be put down.

I checked in on Cody and found him still asleep. I dressed quickly and went straight to Liberty's pen. There was Uncle Neal, sitting with his eagle.

Neal's eyes were moist. It broke my heart to see that bird still plopped there. How hard would it have been, I wondered, after all these weeks, simply to stand up? "Today's the day, isn't it?" I said.

"You heard?"

"Yeah, we've known. Does she have all day at least?"

Neal nodded but didn't speak.

After breakfast I took a call about a hurt raccoon in Woodinville. The man on the phone wouldn't listen to the few questions we always asked, like "Describe the condition of the animal."

"That'll be obvious enough when you get here," he snapped. "I told you, it's hurt."

"Where's the raccoon?"

"In my backyard. Are you coming or not?"

I told Uncle Neal about it. I was sure he'd want to stay with Liberty, but he surprised me. "Let's go," he said grimly.

We went. It turned out to be easy enough to find the raccoon, even without Sage. It was under the man's deck, in agony, crying something awful. The man was a snappy dresser, every hair in place. He was wearing a sweatband; his head was ringed with embroidered golf balls. "What happened?" Neal asked.

"Just kill it," the man told him. "I have a ten-fifteen tee time."

"What happened?" Neal repeated firmly.

"Look at this," the man said. "Look at my hot-tub lid. Pure maliciousness. Maybe the rest will learn to stay out of my yard."

"You need to tell me what happened to the raccoon," Neal insisted, plainly irritated.

The man's forehead was breaking out in a sweat. It was becoming obvious why he wore a headband. "I hit it with a hockey stick, okay? I broke my son's hockey stick, and maybe the miserable creature's back. Just do whatever you do—drag it out and put it down."

Uncle Neal got on his knees and peeked under the deck. "From the looks of it, you did break the raccoon's back. I'm afraid I can't help you, though. I'm not licensed to euthanize animals. Not that I would. Call Animal Control."

"The dogcatchers? Thanks for nothing. Now I'm definitely going to be late. And look what the deer have done to my fruit trees, will you?"

To the side of Uncle Neal's eye, a vein was throbbing. I was afraid he was going to blow a fuse. Voice loaded with tension, Neal said, "From the looks of it, this is a new subdivision."

"Of course it is. So what?"

"Not very long ago it was these animals' home. That raccoon's creek didn't use to run through a concrete culvert. It knew there was water inside your hot tub, even with the lid closed. Just for a second, picture how *you* would like it if somebody bulldozed your community and *your* home. Left you nowhere to live, even in your own backyard."

The man flushed bright red. "You're talking nonsense, mister."

"I understand it. Why can't you?" The voice was Cody's. He'd been standing back, horrified by the nonstop wails from the injured raccoon. "What if giant raccoons destroyed your house and then broke your back with a giant hockey stick?"

The man looked at him strangely. "What are you people, lunatics? I think you should leave now. Mister, I don't know what planet you came from, but you're teaching your kids utter foolishness."

"We're his niece and nephew," I corrected him, "and proud of it. Maybe you should loosen your headband, sir. You must be wearing it too tight."

I couldn't believe I'd just said that. The man was speechless.

Uncle Neal took a deep breath. "Next time, just call me before you do anything, okay?"

We were about to go when Cody burst into tears, just melted down. I got down on my knees, held him, and said, "What is it, Cody?"

"I can't stand the way it's crying," he blubbered.

"I know, I know."

His chest was heaving like it might explode. "Can't we at least take it to a vet?"

Uncle Neal gave in. I put on the heavy coat, the welding gloves, and squeezed under the deck with the net. The raccoon hissed at me, then snarled viciously. "I'm not the enemy," I said. "I've come to help."

I snaked the net forward and tried to work it over the raccoon's back, but there wasn't any clearance between the animal and the deck. It squirmed away, dragging itself in pain.

I cussed under my breath, bellied forward, and tried again. This time I got the net over the raccoon. I started backing up, or trying to. "Pull me by my legs, Cody, if you can reach them."

That helped. I backed out of there dragging the net with me and the raccoon inside it. Cody ran for a carrier. I had to handle the raccoon. It was growling, snarling, and spitting. It wanted to take my head off and I had to hang on tight. It bit the welding gloves again and again. It was horrible to hear an animal in such pain. The golfer was on his way out. "Close the gate behind you," he called.

It was an eerie ride to the vet. The raccoon was in the very back. We couldn't see it, but we sure could hear it. Sage reacted with her ears to every wailing cry. Cody was chewing on his lower lip.

Suddenly there was no sound at all from the back, and Neal said, "Thank goodness."

We caught an early lunch at a Wendy's. We were so subdued. Some small birds, a bunny, a few squirrels, and a snake had died in the ambulance, but they'd done it without a whimper. My mind kept going back and forth between the raccoon and Liberty. Horrible day.

Back at the van, the pager had a number for us to call back. A black bear cub with no mother had been spotted near Coupeville, on Whidbey Island. We took off like a shot. The drive would take two, three hours, depending on the traffic. Cody got out his Game Boy. Another cub for Tyler, I kept thinking. Things were looking up.

We drove north on I-5 halfway to Canada, turned west, then crossed the bridge over Deception Pass onto Whidbey Island. At Deception Pass, the tide was going out like rapids in a river. We would have stopped to look, but we were on the track of a bear.

But by the time we got to Coupeville the cub had taken off. With jets from a nearby navy station roaring overhead, we beat the blackberry thickets, but no luck. Even Sage couldn't find the bear. On our way back we stopped at the tourist pullout to look at Deception Pass. The tide had turned, the waters below were relatively calm, and the sailboats were passing through in both directions. All of a sudden somebody yelled, "Anybody here from Jackie's Wild Seattle? Jackie's Wild Seattle?"

A young couple from Oregon had seen the ambulance in the parking lot, run to the overlook, and found us. Within minutes we were following their van south on Whidbey Island again, this time bound for the cliffs near Ebey's Landing. We were after another orphan, a baby harbor seal.

"Its mother probably left it on the beach while she went fishing," Neal had told them at first. "She'll be back."

The woman had shaken her head emphatically. "We have

a good pair of binoculars. The baby seal has wounds all over its back, like a dog got ahold of it."

At the end of our drive we were standing on the top of the cliff. The baby seal, sixty or seventy feet below, was on one of the few pockets of sand along the narrow and extremely rocky beach.

"Tide's coming in," the woman fretted.

"Sure hope you can find a way down," the man said as they turned to go. "There doesn't appear to be one real close. I wish we could stay, but we're already late."

We couldn't find a route down in either direction. We lost ten minutes trying to find one. Back where we started, we peered over the edge again. Fingers of white water were reaching for the baby seal. "It's going to drown," Cody wailed.

"This is so frustrating," I said to Neal. "I keep thinking about that climbing rope in one of your duffel bags. I only wish you still had your climbing stuff."

Neal ran his hand over his skull, rubbed his chin where his beard used to be. "I still have my stuff, from my search-and-rescue days. Once in a while I use it for an animal rescue. But if you're thinking what I think you're thinking, let's not get carried away."

I crept close to the edge for another look at the features on the cliff below. It wasn't a smooth face by any means. The hard chalky-colored rock had a lot of character to it, ins and outs and cracks and nobs and ledges, and it had a bit of slope to it, which was good. All in all it looked like a free-climbing playground. "Got a climbing harness and a figure eight, Uncle Neal?"

"Got those," he answered reluctantly.

"Is it a standard length rope?"

"Fifty meters. A hundred and sixty-five feet."

"So I can rappel down no problem."

"Maybe, but that's when you *would* have problems. We can't haul the seal up in the carrier. There's no time for all that. The tide's coming in fast, and I'm good as useless up top with only one hand."

"What about that old canvas pack of yours? I can bring the seal up on my back. And I can guess what your problem number two is—me climbing back up without you being able to belay me. Got an ascender, anything I can use for protection on the way up?"

He seemed surprised I was thinking like a climber and talking the lingo.

"I've got jumars," he said reluctantly, "but I doubt you've ever gotten into that at your climbing camp, even the second summer. That's big wall stuff."

"I used jumars last summer, the last day. Lake Placid Search and Rescue was practicing jugging up a rock face, and two of us were invited to join them. All I'll need for protection is one of those jumars. . . . C'mon, Uncle Neal, that baby seal is running out of time."

"I dunno, maybe we should back off. It's just that I've never seen you on a rope before, Shannon."

"She's an ace!" Cody declared.

I laughed. "Like you'd know, Cody. Uncle Neal, I can at least try. There's no end of holds. Give it a look."

Neal gave *me* a look instead, took my measure. He seemed to find something, maybe the look in my eyes, that finally turned his frown into a grin.

"Uncle Neal," I said, "I really believe I can do it. Granted, I haven't climbed a rope with a seal on my back. Will that seal chew my ears off?"

"Doubtful," Neal said, "but not guaranteed. They do look good on you."

"Soooo?"

"Sure would be something to rescue that seal."

"Alrighty then."

16

BACK ON THE ROCK

Neal backed the ambulance toward the edge and stopped about twenty feet short. I tied off to the frame of the van, and Neal inspected my knot. He wasn't taking anything for granted, which was fine by me. I stepped into the climbing harness and snugged it just so. We practiced rigging the jumar for the climb back up. Neal threw the rope over the cliff.

Cody handed me Neal's ancient canvas pack. I tossed the jumar inside with a length of webbing, put the pack on, loosened the shoulder straps, then fastened them across my chest with a carabiner so the pack couldn't fall off my shoulders. Neal's figure eight was exactly the kind of rappelling device I'd used before. I attached it to the harness below my belly button with a locking 'biner. Remembering from my summers at climbing camp, I slowly, carefully fed the rope through the figure eight and clipped it to the locking 'biner.

Neal was watching all this like a hawk. Rappelling is basically easy, but if you get careless and make a mistake in your prep, it's also an easy way to die. When I was all done Neal checked it over once more. "I'm impressed," he announced finally. "You're good to go, Shannon. You're on rappel."

"Rappelling," I answered, like climbers are supposed to do. With that, keeping the rope taut, I backed toward the edge.

When I got there I leaned way back. That's the whole thing, not to be afraid of that unnatural position. A look over my shoulder and I saw the surf break right on the seal. The retreating wave pulled the seal away from the base of the cliff and down onto a gravelly spit between boulders. Another wave that big and the animal would be out to sea and drowning.

Leaning way back, I started feeding rope through the figure eight and went over the edge with small steps. I got a little sideways but adjusted with my legs and kept my balance. Cody was big-eyed. He'd never seen me on a rope before. "This is major," I heard him mutter.

"Beee *goood*," I told him in my best E.T. imitation, and continued walking down the cliff.

When I glanced up again, I was already halfway down. Cody and Neal were both on their bellies looking down at me, huge grins on their faces. Sage, with her tongue hanging out, was watching too. "How's it feel?" Neal called.

"I'm pumped," I called back. "It's good to be back on the rock. I could do this all day!"

"My sister is the greatest sister in the world," I heard Cody say as I dropped some more. I pretended I was out of earshot.

My feet hit the beach. I got off the rope and quickly looked around for the seal. "To your right!" Neal called, and I waded that direction, trying to keep my balance on some slippery kelp. The surf surged around my knees and rocked me, but I stayed upright. This was a scary place to be at high tide. I thought I'd lost the seal for sure when I saw it being carried past me. I reached out and grabbed it.

The baby looked up at me, its huge liquid eyes running with pus. Some of the whiskers were stuck together. It moaned. Suddenly the smell hit me. It was sickly sweet at first but after a few seconds the odor was distinctly putrid. There were deep bites and gashes all over the seal's back, along its sides, too. I turned and waded back with it to the base of the cliff.

"How is it?" Neal called down.

"Pretty bad. Wounds are infected."

"Jackie can give it antibiotics."

"Hear that?" I said to the seal. "No worries. We're going to fix you up."

I set the seal down in the shallow water and pinned it against the cliff with my feet as I got ready for the climb. I put the figure eight away, then brought out the jumar and attached it to the locking 'biner with about eighteen inches of webbing, so the jumar was in front of my chest. Then I fed my end of the climbing rope through the jumar, which was going to be my protection on the way back up. It would suddenly catch and hold tight if I fell.

As fast and as gently as I could, I worked the pack up and around the seal. It was too weak to put up much resistance.

Pack on my back, I clipped the straps together across my chest with a carabiner. I was ready to climb, but the baby seal was heavier than I would have guessed.

It was only then that it hit me: I'd never climbed with weight on my back before. It was going to make a difference, a big difference.

With a hissing rush, a wave caught me all the way to my thighs. I held tight to the cliff and barely avoided going down. The wave pulled back with a rush. The next one would have me swimming. "Time to climb," I said under my breath. I reached for my first holds and boosted myself up with my legs.

Less than ten feet up, I felt the strength pouring out of me like somebody had suddenly pulled the plug. Uh-oh. What did this seal weigh, twenty-five, thirty pounds?

I scanned for the best route. Not just for my next move, but a series of moves that would lead me up and out.

Up I went, reaching for my spots with outstretched fingertips and feet. Whenever possible, I freed a hand and slid the jumar up the rope. If I fell, its teeth would grab the rope, and that was a good feeling.

I looked over my shoulder. The baby seal's face was right next to mine. It was too weak to bite even if it wanted to. The stench was awful. I thought I might be sick.

Man, this was hard. My legs were screaming. No question, it was the hardest thing I'd tried to do in my life. Maybe it was going to be too hard. My forearms were all pumpy; it felt like they were going to cramp.

Get the pack off my back? Drop the seal? Maybe I should. I had such a long way to go and this was too exhausting.

"How you doing?" Neal called.

I found a little ledge for my feet, good handholds, and took the opportunity to rest. "Okay," I panted.

I struggled up as soon I felt some strength come back, but soon got stopped by a difficult spot. I shouldn't have come this way. To the right was better.

I worked my way right. Here was a route, but this was getting way hard. I might as well have been carrying a load of rocks.

Maybe I would have to give it up.

Maybe I would.

Suddenly I was picturing Neal with his thumb about sliced off and refusing to give up on that red-tailed hawk.

I just had to dig deeper.

"Go, Shannon, you can do it!" Cody called.

"I'm not sure about that," I muttered, not that he could hear me.

With every ounce of strength I had, I kept climbing. To make things worse, the weight of the seal kept shifting from side to side, and the sick baby kept whimpering. It was hard to bear, how much pain it was in.

"Shannie's a lot stronger than she looks," I heard from above. This from my little brother as my muscles were cramping and I was sucking wind.

"Shannon, you're nearly halfway up," Neal called. I could hear it in his voice. He knew the real score, how much trouble I was having.

I looked up and said, "This is tougher than I thought. I might have to drop the pack."

"Take it one step at a time," Neal said. "Drop it if you have to. No question in my mind, though, you can do it."

I could tell he wasn't just saying it. My uncle really meant it. Unlike me, he had known how hard this was going to be from the first. And he thought I could do it.

That meant something. It meant a lot.

I thought about everything Neal could still do even though he was sick, and here I was, healthy as a horse. It would feel pretty incredible if I could bring this seal up to the top of the cliff.

My mind cleared. Think how strong you are, I told myself, not how weak. Quit looking up at those guys on top. Keep your eyes on your route, on your holds. Close your eyes when you're resting, stay calm, stay steady.

There, that feels better. Listen to the wind, the ocean, the gulls. Who would have thought you'd ever be in a place like this doing anything like this?

Somehow I kept climbing. Finally their faces were in my near vision. Fifteen feet to go, and I was running on empty. "You're nearly here," Neal said.

"I've made a discovery. Seals are made out of lead."

"Don't give up," Cody said.

"No way," I told him. "I'm just resting."

It was time for the last push, at an angle up to the left. "I'm coming up," I told them. "Nothing's stopping me now."

I don't know what it was—adrenaline, I guess. My booster rockets kicked in. Finally I lifted myself one last time and felt the grip of Neal's good hand like a skyhook. I was on top and so was the seal.

I stayed on my hands and knees while they got the pack and the seal off. Then I collapsed onto my back, panting. I rolled my eyes one way and then the other. The sky swam. The earth felt so good and solid underneath me.

"Awesome," Uncle Neal said. "Happy, Shannon?"

"Yeah, happy and exhaustionized."

"That's not a word," Cody objected.

"It is now."

We transferred the moaning seal baby to a carrier and sped off. Neal said she was real sick. I was so pumped about her living, I didn't see how I could stand it if she didn't, and that's when I remembered Liberty.

It was four o'clock in the afternoon. By the time we got back home, well, I didn't even want to think about it.

Cody fell asleep on the drive back. Neal stopped for gas at Mount Vernon. I went to the back of the van to check up on the seal. She wasn't moving. At first I told myself she was just resting, but I knew better. She was dead.

I wouldn't have told Neal, but he came around to look. Cody woke up and came back too. None of us was even able to cry. "It's not fair," Cody said. "She was just a baby." You do everything you can, I thought, but sometimes death still wins.

The ride back was real quiet. Neal had to be thinking about Liberty, and I was fretting about my parents. It had been almost two weeks since we'd heard from them.

When we got back to the center I got on the computer right away. Cody was looking over my shoulder. There it was, a new message from my mother.

How I wished Cody hadn't been there. After a paragraph of chitchat, my mother casually dropped a bomb. My father had gone into Afghanistan.

I thought about closing down the message real fast. A glance over my shoulder and I could see the damage had already been done. The little bugger always reads the last part first.

Not to worry, Cody and Shannon. Your father has been at a refugee camp in Afghanistan for about ten days now. He'll be fine, the war was over last December. The peacekeeping forces are right there at the refugee camp where he's working. They really, really needed him. We'll be home in a month. Don't you worry, okay?

Cody started to cry. I was numb. I had to find a way to reassure him. How was it my parents had thought I was up to this job?

"Afghanistan," Cody whispered. "I can't believe it. It's full of land mines there, everybody knows that."

"Not in the refugee camps, Cody."

"Afghanistan is where they trained the terrorists, the ones that flew the planes into the World Trade Center."

"I know, but they're history."

"No they aren't, some of them are still hiding."

He was right, of course. There was no point in saying he wasn't. I put my arm around him—he was trembling—and said, "We just have to keep the faith."

My baby brother collapsed into my arms, his head against my chest. Hold him, I thought, hold him close. He needs his mother, and I'm the next best thing.

Suddenly we heard our names being called, ours and Neal's. It was Jackie, and this was urgent, whatever it was.

Still dazed, we stepped outside the office. What now? Then I remembered Liberty. Not more bad news. I didn't think we could take it.

Neal was coming out of the house. He slowly closed the door behind him. Jackie rushed over and embraced him. "Neal, you aren't going to believe this." There were tears in her eyes, tears of joy.

"What is it?" he asked cautiously.

"Liberty's on her feet! Come see."

Cody and I followed them as Jackie took the shortcut through the service gate. Sure enough, Liberty was standing up. The eagle looked so different, so much bigger and so puffed out, so alive. She was walking around the big flying enclosure, looking all around.

Neal went in and sat down on the gravel. His bald eagle walked right over to him, and they looked into each other's eyes. They were nose to beak, that close.

"I've seen a lot," Jackie said, shaking her head. "This is right up there. Death was winning, no doubt about it. But not this time. Not this time."

I squeezed Cody's hand and he squeezed back. He looked up at me. "Everything is going to be okay, Shannie, isn't it?"

17

A WHOLE DIFFERENT FROG

Liberty had a future now, at least as one of Jackie's distinguished guests, but Neal had something more ambitious in mind. He told me that Jackie used to have an eagle she could take to school programs. "Wouldn't it be something if Liberty could do that for Jackie? Be an ambassador for the whole animal kingdom?"

"She'd have to be trained, right?"

"It would be a long shot. Most eagles don't have the disposition for it—not just the training, but being around so many people. The first step is to get her used to the glove."

The heavy falconer's glove reached almost to Neal's elbow. That first day, when Neal extended his good arm into her cage, Liberty wouldn't get onto the glove at all. The second day it was like, Okay, I'll step on your arm but only with one foot. The third day it was, Okay, I'll use both feet but only for a second. The fourth day it was, Yeah, you can take me partway out of my cage, then I'll jump right back in. Finally it was, Okay, I'll let you walk around with me on your arm. Hey, this is fun!

We got another call from Whidbey Island, about that same orphaned bear cub near Coupeville. I was determined to bring it back home this time no matter what. As soon as the call came in I ran to tell Tyler. He flashed a killer smile and said, "I'll tell Gnarly that a buddy is on the way."

"Gnarly?" I teased.

"Not that he knows his name. I can't talk to him. Gotta keep him wild."

"What will you name the other cub, if we get lucky?"

"I guess I'd wait until I see what it's like. Say, don't let the cub's size fool you. Pound for pound, bears are stronger than you would believe."

"Forget everything I know about teddy bears?"

"Definitely."

"Thanks for the tip. You'll come to visit me in the hospital?"

"I didn't mean to—"

I gave him a nudge. "Just kidding, Tyler."

I took him seriously. On the way to Whidbey Island, I made Neal stop to buy a goalie's mask to add to my rescue outfit.

The old woman who met us lived alone about a mile out of Coupeville. Her vegetables and flowers were her pride and joy. The cub had rampaged like a hurricane through parts of her garden.

Her black lab was on guard in front of a big open shed. We went to look before we let Sage out of the ambulance. The lab started barking as we approached, but not at us. The dog was going nuts.

A big wooden pole in the middle of the shed supported

the roof. The cub, the spitting image of Gnarly except for a bigger white patch on its chest, was up above the rafters and clinging to the pole, snarling and growling at the dog below.

The first thing we did was have Mrs. Pasqualetti take her dog away. Then I suited up Sage with her flak jacket.

"Gonna be tricky," Neal said, looking up at the cub. "Too bad there's no door on this shed. That cub can move faster than you'll ever guess, but you've got Sage on your side."

With the heavy coat over a life jacket for extra padding, I looked like the Pillsbury Doughboy accessorized with welding gloves and a hockey mask. All in all, I looked utterly ridiculous. Fortunately no one had a camera.

It was a warm day and I was cooking as I started up the ladder. The idea was to scare the cub down. Mrs. Pasqualetti was back from confining her dog in her basement. She asked unhelpfully, "How many times have you done this, dear?"

"I'm making this up as I go," I said. "Back up, Cody, so the bear doesn't jump on you."

When I stuck my head up above the rafters, the cub sort of screeched, sort of growled, sort of whined. "You'll starve to death if you don't come home with us," I said, but I wasn't speaking the bear's language.

"You sure are cute," I said. "Nice nose, cute face, darling ears. Your teeth, though, they look awfully sharp." Now I really had it riled up. "Don't be such a whiner, you big baby."

Neal moved everybody, including Sage, out of the cub's view. "Coming after you, little bear," I said. "Like it or not."

I climbed into the peak of the shed. As I stepped to straddle two joists, I hit my head and saw stars. It felt like I'd been stabbed in the skull. "Doing all right?" Neal called.

I waited a few seconds, teeth clenched until the pain began to clear. "Sure is warm up here," I said. "Okay, Teddy, I'm coming after you. You're supposed to bail out, okay?"

The bear was about ten feet away. I wished I had something to shove at it, maybe a rake, to get it moving. But it would take time to round up a rake. Crouching, I started toward the cub. I was convinced I was scary enough to scare off Godzilla.

The last thing I would have expected to happen, happened. The teddy sprang from the pole, front legs outstretched, and right onto me, fastening onto my jacket with its sharp claws. I had this screaming, terrified, angry bear on my chest and no clue. Fortunately, thinking was not required. Up went one hand to protect my throat and I raked the other hand down, sweeping the bear off my chest with more strength than I knew I had.

The cub clung to the joists for a second, then shinnied down the pole. It hit the ground running. From the corner of my vision I saw Sage dart in and head it off.

As quickly as I could, I climbed down the ladder and joined the fray.

"You all right, Shan?" my little brother yelled, carrier in hand.

"Never better," I yelled back, and stalked toward the cub. It was darting this way and that. Sage met every zig with a zag. Her flak jacket was taking flak; she was using her side like a backstop.

By now we were in the middle of the vegetable garden. Too bad for the cherry tomatoes. The cub seemed to be tiring, though; it might have been weak from hunger. I saw my chance and leaped. I had it pinned to the ground.

"Awesome, Shannie," I heard Cody yell, and then he was

right there with the carrier, placing it by the bear's angry face, all growls and needle-sharp teeth. I let up a little, felt it squirm toward the carrier. I let up a little more. It had nowhere to go but inside.

Neal helped me up, and that was that. Off came the goalie's mask. I felt like I'd been inside a sauna for three hours and beaten with a stick. I threw off the coat—shredded down the front—and started unbuckling the life jacket. I was dripping with sweat but seemingly intact underneath. The top of my head was still pounding. "Would you like some milk and cookies now?" Mrs. Pasqualetti inquired.

When we got to the center I told Tyler, who was awed at the sight of the cub and looking at me like I'd hit the ball out of the park, that he didn't have to think of a name for the little she-bear. I already had it: Sweetness.

Tyler and I watched as Gnarly and Sweetness met. They were on either side of the guillotine door separating the rooms of the bear den. No fur flew. The cubs were real cautious of each other, real interested. Sweetness went to a far corner when Big Bear, Tyler, brought in a huge bowl of fruit salad. Big Bear left and Sweetness made short work of the fruit. On the clinic side of the door to the bear den, Tyler took the head off his costume, held it under his arm like a football, and gave me a bear hug. "Now they've got each other," he said. I'd never seen Tyler happy like that. I only wished Neal hadn't gone straight to Liberty, that he'd seen this instead.

The next day took us to the foothills of the Cascades. A hiker had come across a raven caught in leg-hold traps.

"Traps?" Neal asked me as we got under way. "More than one? You're sure they said traps?"

"I can't explain it," I said. "That's what I heard."

When we got there it was obvious enough. The raven had been trying to get at a piece of meat suspended over two steel leg-hold traps camouflaged under the pine needles. These traps were supposed to be illegal. Hopping around and trying to get at the bait, the raven had stepped into one trap and then the other.

The big black bird was a pitiful sight. One leg had been shattered and almost severed. The other leg Uncle Neal had hopes for. The trap had caught it high on the drumstick where there was quite a bit of meat to protect the bone.

"I don't get it," Cody said. "Why would people want to catch ravens?"

The bird kept eyeing us, head cocked to the side, black eyes flicking. No doubt it figured we were there to kill it.

"Probably it was coyotes or bobcats they were after," Neal said. "A lot of the time they end up catching somebody's dog, or an eagle, or who-knows-what."

"Look at that beak," Cody said. "Shannon, it's huge. That raven could hurt you bad."

"I'll wear gloves. Too bad my hockey mask is back at Jackie's. How strong is that bill, Neal?"

"You don't want to find out. Talk nice to Raven. This one might have been unlucky, but he's way smart. They live year-round from the arctic to the deserts of Arizona. What other bird can do that? Raven stole the sun to light the earth, stole the moon and the stars, too."

Cody was all confused. "From who?"

"From an old man who kept them in a box. The world was completely dark before then. Raven invented mosquitoes, too. Known for his tricky sense of humor."

Cody was eyeing the bird in the traps. None of this was adding up.

"Sounds like stories," I suggested to Cody.

"You bet," Neal said enthusiastically. "Native American stories. Raven's the star of lots of them. He's a clever hunter, too. Up north—I'm talking about real life now—he's known to lead wolves to moose. When the wolf pack brings down the moose, the raven eats."

By now I had the gloves on and my courage up. After Sweetness, I was ready for anything. Neal coached me on how to open the jaws of the trap.

Neal and Cody backed off as I approached the big shaggy-throated bird, talking softly. "I've come to help you, Raven," I said as soothingly as possible. "Please don't hurt me. I'm extremely attached to my body as it is. Hey, you're some bird."

As I knelt, the raven flinched, cocked its shiny head, and looked at me sharply. I was afraid it would struggle in the traps and hurt itself even more. It didn't.

On my knees, I went to work and freed the bird from those nasty traps. Strange, but I could have done it without gloves. That raven never went for me even once. As I released the second leg, the less injured one, I covered the bird lightly with one of my legs so it wouldn't fly. Then I took the raven in my arms, and into Cody's carrier it went.

We hurried to the closest vet who worked with Jackie. It turned out to be Dr. Minorca, who'd operated on Liberty. She amputated the leg that was hanging on by a thread, at the knee, if that's what you call it. There was already a good chance that infection had set in, so she started the raven on antibiotics. Dr. Minorca said they were tough birds, and our raven, a male, would probably survive. We could come back for him in a couple of days.

Back at the center, working with Liberty, Neal mentioned

that he was going to have to find someone else to help train her. "How come?" I asked.

"It can't just be me. She has to get used to working with other people. It can't be I'm the only one or she'll never be able to go on the road for Jackie. You know that bald eagle on the side of the van? When Liberty grows into her white plumage, I've got this idea that everywhere she goes, people will figure that's her."

"Let Tyler work with her," I said without hesitating.

Neal looked stunned, wounded in the heart.

"Yes, Tyler," I insisted. "Trust me on this, Uncle Neal. He's in the clinic right now, cleaning cages. Go talk to him about it."

I was pleasantly surprised to see he was thinking about it. He was slowly turning it over. At last Neal said, "You sure about this?"

"Positive."

"You want to come with me to talk to him?"

"I don't think so. This has to be between you and him. I never gave you the idea, okay?"

So far so good, but I was so afraid Tyler would turn him down. Tyler might say no out of reflex, just because he was so wary of Neal and not good with people to begin with.

I gave them ten minutes, then peeked. The two of them were together in the enclosure. The falconer's glove was on Tyler's hand.

Now it's your turn, Liberty, I thought. Come through for *me* this time. I was crossing my fingers so hard. It took fifteen or twenty long minutes before the eagle stepped from her perching branch onto the glove for Tyler. Quickly, she stepped back. It took another ten minutes for her to step onto the glove again, but this time she stayed on. Tyler walked her slowly around the pen, pretty as you please.

This had taken some bravery on Tyler's part, no question about it, on account of Neal and on account of the bird. With her bill, she could have put his eye out so fast. Tyler's expression was as serious as could be. Eventually the grim line of his mouth changed to a faint smile. He was pretty proud of himself.

I'd been sitting and watching for so long, I'd forgotten all about Cody. I got up feeling uneasy and started looking around. Inside the clinic, no one had seen him. I was getting more and more concerned as I started checking the grounds. He was nowhere to be found.

An hour and maybe more had gone by since I'd seen him. I was just about frantic. I stopped to think, then ran toward the creek. It was the only other place I could think of.

There he was, just climbing out of the creek with his backpack in his hand. Ever since he'd heard about Dad being in Afghanistan, well, I had been expecting some sort of upset feelings episode. "Cody!" I practically screamed. "Don't scare me like that!"

He hung his head. "Sorry, Shan, I couldn't find you."

"That didn't mean you could go off by yourself. I thought we had an agreement."

"I had to catch one of those frogs."

"Oh," I said, trying to calm down. "Did you catch one, then?"

"Not really."

"What does that mean?"

"I let it go."

"Well, good."

I made him promise not to disappear on me like that ever again. Promise or no promise, I was going to have to watch him like a hawk.

The next morning Cody slept in, which was unusual. I went to rouse him. Something gross was squashed flat next to him, a very dead frog. "Cody," I said, "what is this road-kill doing in your bed?"

The poor kid was stricken. "Aw, Shannie, is he dead? He was alive when I put him in there last night."

"Cody, I thought you told me you let the frog go."

"I did. This was a whole different frog."

18

TYLER AND LIBERTY

Every day or two Tyler and I visited on "the talking stump," as we called it. He was smiling a lot these days, and it looked good on him. "Your uncle says animals all have their individual personalities. He said he didn't know about insects. I asked him if Jackie ever rehabbed ants and he said no, but once she rehabbed a butterfly."

"You and Neal are really getting along, aren't you?"

"Yeah," Tyler said, "he's all right."

I asked Tyler if he knew about Neal being treated for cancer. He did, and he was surprised that I knew. I told him how I'd found out, and that Cody still didn't know. Tyler promised not to tell—and I trusted him.

Tyler was around the center more lately, six hours a day instead of four, so there were more chances for us to get together. He'd told his father he was working longer hours to get it over with faster, but he told me the real reason was that he liked being at the center, liked the bear cubs crawling over him, liked training the eagle with Neal.

I figured out what Tyler didn't say: whatever time he spent at the center he didn't have to spend handing wrenches to his father. Well, and then there was me, I guess. I was somebody he could talk to.

One day as we were sitting on the stump Tyler came out with, "Three more years. Three more years."

I couldn't tell if something had happened at home, but he looked desperate to talk. "Until what?" I asked tentatively.

"Until I can get away. Until I'm out of high school, and eighteen. My dad thinks I'll work at the shop with him, inherit the business one day and all that. There's no way. I can't tell him that, but there's no way."

"Why can't you tell him?"

"He'd make me pay for it every day. So I let him think it's a possibility. The day after I'm out of high school, I'm out of here. I'm on a bus."

"A bus to where?"

"I don't know. The army?"

"What about college?"

"Me, college?"

"Why not? Why not you?"

He seemed pleased I was even thinking of him that way, but his smile morphed into a frown. "No way. Anyway, they couldn't afford it. If I need anything from him, it's hopeless."

"What about your mother? You never mention her."

"That's hopeless too. She won't ever stand up to him. She just can't do it. My mom just tries to get from one day to the next."

"If you ask me, your family should have counseling, not just you."

He laughed a desperate sort of laugh. "We did that earlier this summer. Three sessions, and it was torture. My dad just sat there like it was all *my* problem. I couldn't come out with what it's like at home—all the tension, all about how mean and sarcastic he is. As soon as we were out of sight of the counselor, he would've made me pay. My mother just sat there. She'd been through it years before—he used to beat her up. She just doesn't want it to get worse again. My mom gave up a long time ago."

"The therapist you see now, is it the same one or different?"

"Different guy. He keeps asking me where my anger comes from, and I'm like, 'Duh. . . . ' It's a farce, Shannon. I can't just come out and tell him what he wants to know."

"Which is . . . ?"

"Which is what it was like when I—you know, the dog, the whole thing about the dog. Why I did it, what I was feeling, what was behind it. If I talked about the big picture, it would get back somehow to my father, and my mother and I would have to pay."

His words hung in the air for a while. I didn't know how much more of this I wanted to hear. I wasn't sure I should get more involved than I already was, and this was the moment to back off.

The thing is, it was obvious how badly he needed someone to talk to. Hoping for the best, I kept going. "You can tell me," I said. "You should get it out, Tyler. It won't get back to him, don't worry about that."

He looked at me desperately.

"Really," I said. "You should tell me."

"Okay, then. Every time it happened—when I'd take out my rage, as the therapist calls it—the tension had been building up at home to where I just couldn't take it."

"It wasn't only that one time, with that one dog?"

"That one dog, but not that one time. The dog and I went way back. Six months, anyway. That creature would always come back, like my shadow or something. Unclipped, medium-sized poodle, leaves and junk hanging off it, fur in its eyes, disgustingly slinky, 'fraidy-cat kind of dog. Always cringing like you were about to hit it. Obviously it had been hit before, somewhere else. It was a stray. It always came around to our place because my mom would feed it."

"You talk like it gave you the creeps."

"It did. It was one of those smiley dogs. He'd cringe and smile, flop down and show you his belly. It was pathetic how lame he was. I couldn't stand him, his weakness. I started kicking him, and still he'd come around. Hit him with things, he'd still come around. The dog accepted it, expected it. *Liked* me, if you can believe it. Sometimes, after school and before my mom got home, it would be just me and the poodle. My dad would be at the shop, a stone's throw away. He knew it was going on, didn't care. He thought the dog was pathetic too. He was amused that it made me so crazy."

"Why do you think it did?"

"Oh, I've had some time to think about that. It's all mixed up with the stuff my dad would say to me, how lame I was, how weak I was. When my mother isn't around, my dad lays it on especially thick. I'd stalk off—him yelling things at me. I'd go down to the creek, and wouldn't you know that poodle would follow me. I'd turn around and whack the dog. It'd cringe, take another whack. Just like me. I can't tell you how many times I thought I better just hit the road, but I never did."

"How come?"

" 'Cuz of what I knew that would do to my mother. I'm all she's got. I leave, it would just be her and him. Scary thought. That last time at the creek . . ."

He stopped, his face all contorted.

"Go ahead and tell me, Tyler."

"I was so messed up—head buzzing, everything white-hot—I couldn't see straight. I picked up a long smooth stick, maybe a walking stick somebody had dropped. It was really stout. The poodle was smiling, cringing, the usual . . . I just lost it, came down on him hard, broke his back."

I winced. I couldn't look Tyler in the face. "That's awful," was all I managed to say.

"It got worse. Now the creature's in unbelievable agony, but he's not dead. Crying at the top of his lungs."

"I heard a raccoon in pain like that this summer. I'll never forget it."

"Now what do I do? I panicked. I shoved him into the creek, waded after him, pushed him down with the stick until he drowned. There, I said it. Now you think I'm a monster."

Dead silence made the air so heavy I could barely breathe. "I don't," I said finally. "I'm sorry it happened. I'm sorry you did it, that you have to live with it, but I don't think that's who you are or who you want to be. I can see how hard you're trying to be different from your father."

He looked me in the eye. "That's it, Shannon. I really don't want to be like him. He's just so cruel, that's all I can call it. Every so often he can't control his temper at all. We had a dog when I was little, a puppy. I watched him club it to death. All it did was chew up something of his. Like father, like son, right? All I know is, it's up to me. I have to get better on my own. That's what I've decided. This summer, at the center, it's the first time I ever felt like I had a chance."

At last I was able to look him in the eye without looking away. "I can tell that you're getting better, Tyler. If you ask me, it's obvious."

"Thanks," he said. "It's not going to work, though."

"Why not?"

"My father notices everything. He knows I'm getting better too, and the weird thing is, he doesn't want me to."

"Are you sure? Sure you aren't being too hard on him?"

Tyler was fighting tears. "I wish. The truth is, my dad wants to drag me down with him, *be* like him. There's no fairy tale ending here, Shannon. My father is like a volcano, only he doesn't wait a thousand years between blowups. Three more years sounds like eternity."

"Just hang in there," I encouraged him. "And tell somebody if it's getting too bad. Maybe Jackie . . ."

"That's the last thing she needs."

"Your therapist, then."

Tyler's break was over. He had to get back to meet up with Neal. As we climbed down from the talking stump he said, "When you go back to New Jersey, at least I'll still have Liberty to talk to. Don't worry, Shannon, I'll hang in there."

Sometimes Tyler and Neal worked with Liberty together, and this was one of those days. I watched from the bench just outside the pen. The way it worked, Liberty would walk off her perch onto Neal's arm, and he'd talk to her and walk around with her on his arm, then let her step back onto her perch. Then she'd do the same with Tyler. Only with Tyler, for a long time she'd lean away from him, like, I don't really want to be doing this, but if Neal thinks I have to, I will.

This was the day Liberty actually perched upright on Tyler's arm. Go, Tyler! I thought, but I didn't want to say anything too embarrassing.

When I saw Tyler the next day he was fresh from another session with the eagle. He told me that Liberty had even leaned toward him a little, like she did with Neal. Liberty actually looked him in the eye, for a long time. Tyler was pumped. "Shannon, you wouldn't believe what it's like with that huge bird on your arm. I mean, you have to hold your arm out perfectly straight. It helps if you dig your elbow into your side. You take a walk around the whole rehab path with her, a couple hundred yards, and you wonder how long you'll be able to hold out. And I mean, I'm strong. It'll be awesome when her tail feathers and the feathers on her head turn white. That will be something to see."

What made the best watching was when Liberty started walking from Neal's arm onto Tyler's and back. Liberty thought that was a pretty good trick, and so did the guys. They were also getting her used to her jesses, the leather straps around her feet. With jesses she could be leashed to her handler or to a perch. It was part of what she would need to become a bird Jackie could show at her programs. Jackie usually took her favorite red-tailed hawk, but she could take them both, and the bald eagle would be even more impressive. Jackie was talking about Tyler handling the eagle for school programs and so on. When the time came, his father would get behind the idea, she was fairly sure.

"In my dreams," Tyler said.

19

CRY TIDNAB

Our raven was back from the vet. Among all the noisy birds inside the clinic, he didn't have a thing to say. Cody spent a lot of time with him, talking to him, trying to get him to talk back. "He's my Liberty," my brother whispered in my ear. The raven's stump was healing into a hard, leathery knot, and the bird began to put weight on it. Cody gave him a name, Kickstand, for the way he leaned. The name was an instant hit with the volunteers. We wondered if Kickstand would stand a chance in the wild with only one foot. Jackie didn't know. "We'll give him the chance," she said.

When the time came, Cody was given the honor of moving Kickstand to the flying pen next to Liberty's. I went along to watch. Cody set the carrier down in the middle of the enclosure, undid the latch, and ceremoniously swung the carrier door open.

At just that moment a gust of wind came up, and it opened another door, the one to the flying pen.

One hop and Kickstand was airborne. With an agile twist of his wings, one up and one down, the raven flew through sideways as the door was swinging shut. He'd nearly been clipped, but he was free and gaining altitude. "Oh no," Cody cried. "Kickstand, come back!"

Kickstand hadn't flown far. He was high in a cedar looking down on us. *Cr-r-ruck*, he called. *Prruk! Prruk! Tok! Kla-wock!*

"Wow, Cody," I said. "Your friend suddenly has a lot to say."

Cody's head was craned way back. It was like his eyes were never going to leave that bird. "Look how he's leaning on that branch with his stump, Shannie. Do you think he's going to be okay?"

"Looks to me like he doesn't need any more rehab."

"Do you think he'll stick around?"

"I guess you better say good-bye. He might fly away any second."

Cody didn't say good-bye, and as it turned out, Kickstand didn't fly away.

The raven had to invent a new way to make landings, and it was awkward at first. He'd grasp a branch with the talons of his good foot and lean on his stump, all the while beating his wings for balance.

In a day or two Kickstand's landings were almost smooth, yet he was still hanging around the center, maybe because Cody was feeding him, not to mention all the stealing he did from the deer and the coyotes, the ducks and geese, the sea otter, the raccoons, the possums, and the skunks. Kickstand was a glutton, and he also had a mischievous streak. The raven especially enjoyed dropping small rocks through the roof mesh onto the mountain lion's head.

Neal said that ravens have about fifty different calls, but Kickstand seemed to have a hundred. He could even bark like a dog. He made the most wonderful gurgling and popping sounds, but most often would sit high in a cedar and go *tok-tok-tok*.

Out on the driveway in the front of the office, Kickstand enjoyed messing with the golden retrievers. The raven would play wounded, then fly away at the last second when the dogs rushed him. Sage, as I might have guessed, declined to participate.

One day Kickstand stole the keys to the ambulance off the porch railing where Neal had set them. With the keys in his bill, the raven flew straight as an arrow over Jackie's house, circled once, then came in low and dropped them down her chimney. After circling one more time, croaking loudly, he landed on the chimney and laughed his shaggy-throated head off.

Amazingly, Kickstand would come to Cody. My brother soon had the big bird eating out of his hand, perching on his arm, roosting on his shoulder. This was a new one for Jackie. The volunteers were taking pictures. Kickstand taught Cody how to talk raven, or at least that's what Cody claimed. The two of them would go to opposite ends of the center, a couple hundred yards apart, and carry on a so-called conversation. Cody told me he'd learned a few "dangerous things" from the raven.

"Like what?" I challenged him.

"Sure you want to know?"

"Try me."

"Well, for one thing, this land Jackie built on used to be the core of a volcano bigger than Rainier."

"No kidding," I said.

"I'm serious, Shan. There's still a lot of power here. The whole place could explode at any moment."

"Is that so," I said. "Any telling when?"

"No, but there's one place where the energy is more powerful than anywhere else."

"And where's that?"

"In the middle of Sasha's pen."

"Really?"

"Kickstand told me that if you go into the lion's pen and hold your hands above your shoulders . . . your head will explode."

That last part he'd said in a hush. "I guess I won't try it," I said. "Seems to me, before you could lift your hands above your head, that cougar would rip your lungs out."

"You're dead meat either way," Cody said. "Promise you won't try it."

"Alrighty then," I said. "I guess I won't."

A baby raccoon went missing inside the clinic. As Rosie was transferring a batch of them into a carrier so their cage could be cleaned, it squirmed out of her hands and was off to the races.

Rosie almost had it a couple of times, but then the baby raccoon hid, maybe among the little animal houses stacked everywhere, possibly under or behind the washer and dryer or one of the refrigerators. It could have been in any of a thousand places. For a while we all got on our hands and knees, Jackie, half a dozen volunteers, and Cody and me, but the little bandit was lying low.

"This is a job for Sage," Cody announced when we were all thoroughly frustrated. "Sage could find that raccoon in a minute."

Jackie shook her head. "No way," she said. "Think of all the different smells in here, Cody. With hundreds of birds and mammals, including all those other raccoons, even Sage couldn't find it."

"Bet ya," he said. He was getting that impossible-to-deal-with look.

I sided with Jackie. "Sage is amazing, but not that amazing."

Now it was the hurt look. "I can't believe you just said that, Shannie. You're the one she's working with now on the rescues!"

Jackie, Rosie, and the volunteers were enjoying this. I looked from them back to the kid. "Okay," I said, "I'll get Sage."

Sage wondered what was up when I called her into the clinic. The retrievers followed, hoping the invitation applied to them. "Sorry," I had to tell them. They went back to the shade on the office porch.

"Here she is, Cody. Now how is this supposed to work?"

"I got an idea. You follow me, and Sage will follow you."

"Then what?"

"You'll see."

I followed Cody over to the baby raccoons' cage, the one that hadn't been cleaned yet. So did Jackie and the volunteers. This was a welcome break from the endless cleaning and feeding and preparing of medications.

The cage was ripe with the smells of fur and food and baby raccoon droppings. Cody grabbed it and set it down on the floor next to Sage, who was looking around but mostly at me, as if I might give her a clue what this was all about.

"I get to say it," Cody declared.

"Say what?"

He stood up and whispered in my ear, "What if all these people hear the code word for raccoon?"

"I think that's okay, Cody. We'll make them swear on a stack of Bibles never to say it."

"Well, I guess that's okay."

My little brother got down on the floor next to Sage, and then he reached into the cage and collected droppings and bits of fur. He passed a handful back and forth between him and the border collie's nose, and then he shouted, "*Tidnab*, Sage, *tidnab*!"

Sage's ears went straight up, and she looked from Cody to me, and me back to Cody. From her nose to the tip of her tail, Sage was suddenly a live wire. She looked doubtfully at Cody, as if it couldn't be true that he knew the code word. She hesitated.

Cody held the handful under his own nose and sniffed. "*Tidnab!*" Cody shouted. "*Tidnab*, Sage!"

With that, Sage shot through my legs and into the laundry room, then into the food prep room, then into the baby mammals room, and finally to the baby birds room, all in less than a minute. When we caught up with her she was dancing on the linoleum under the starlings and the crows.

By now Rosie and Jackie and all the volunteers had arrived. Sage was dancing and whining and looking up, up above the stacks of bird condos, toward some shelves stacked with spare bird cages and cardboard boxes and who knows what.

"I already looked up there," Jackie said.

Cody shook his head dramatically. "That raccoon's up there, I guarantee it."

Jackie was amused. "Would you like to place a bet of

some kind on this, Cody?"

"I sure would. You win, I do the dishes tonight. I win, I get the Swedish meatballs Shanine put away in the refrigerator last night."

Swedish meatballs? It was news to me that Cody liked meatballs. The reason we had leftovers was because he hadn't eaten any.

By this time one of the volunteers had fetched the stepladder. Sage was still in the alert position, eyes like laser beams on a spot directly above.

Cody raced up the ladder, peeked behind an old Radio Shack box, then looked down at us like the cat that's eaten the canary. "Gloves, please."

Half a minute later he was on his way down the stepladder, baby raccoon in hand.

Just then a very big, red-faced man in overalls more or less burst through the clinic door. "Where's Tyler?" he demanded.

"Hi, Gary," Jackie said.

A hush descended over the clinic. Tyler's dad glared at the baby raccoon squirming in Cody's hands, at Sage, at me, at Jackie.

"He's out back," Jackie said. "Working with a bald eagle. You should see them."

"Take me to him," Mr. Tucker said gruffly.

I followed, hanging well back. Tyler's father didn't even look at the animals as he followed Jackie through the clinic. He kept his eyes straight ahead.

Outside, he started looking around, surprised maybe at the scale of it all. If I had to guess, I'd say he'd never been there before. He stopped for a second and took a long look at the plywood fence hiding the bears' den. Then I remembered that Tyler had been telling him about the cubs.

Three steps behind Jackie, Tyler's dad stalked the path that led through the owls, the falcons, and the hawks, and on to the eagles. The last of the eagle enclosures, where Jackie halted, was Liberty's. The heavy tread of Mr. Tucker's boots on the gravel path went silent. He stood there with his hands on his hips.

Kickstand started croaking from a nearby cedar. The croak changed to his *tok-tok-tok*, then to his barking dog routine. Mr. Tucker shot an annoyed glance at the raven.

Unaware of all this, Tyler had his back toward Jackie and his father. "Tyler," Jackie said, and Tyler swiveled slowly toward her, a smile on his face and the big bird on his arm. When Tyler saw his father standing right there, the smile vanished instantly. Liberty must have felt how startled Tyler was. The eagle jumped to the ground, holding one wing stiffly and flapping the other.

"Need you at the shop," Mr. Tucker grunted. "Now."

Jackie stepped in to take care of Liberty and Tyler took off behind his father. Tyler never saw me; his eyes were on the ground. It was just as well. I could only imagine how humiliating this was for him.

It was over as quickly as it started. Everybody was standing around stunned, unsure what to make of Gary Tucker's sudden appearance and equally sudden departure. Everybody was standing around except Cody.

Where was Cody?

20

SLEEPLESS IN SEATTLE

I ran into the house, and that's where I found Cody. He was in the kitchen offering Sage a Swedish meatball. Sage nosed it, pushed it around in Cody's hand, then gently took it into her mouth. Cody touched the back of her head ever so softly, then sort of scratched it, and Sage didn't pull away. She was actually letting Cody pet her.

"Victory," Cody said in a loud whisper. His eyes were popping out of his head. "I figured I had to find a way to prove myself to her, and I did it. She knew I believed in her, that she could find the raccoon. That's the *whole reason* she thinks I'm okay now."

"You sure it wasn't the meatball?"

"Shan, we're lucky we don't have a dad like Tyler's."

"No kidding."

"Kickstand could tell he was a bad man."

"You really think so?"

"I'm pretty sure. Do you believe that animals can tell if a

disaster is going to strike? In my book, it says sometimes dogs can tell that an earthquake is coming."

"I've heard about that. Sure, I believe that's for real."

My brother's forehead was wrinkled with some Deep Thought. He hesitated, then spit it out. "Do you think it's possible to make something happen just by thinking about it?"

"Sure. I think I'm going to milk Jackie's goats, and then I do it."

"Not like that," Cody said impatiently. "I mean, you wish something bad would happen, and then it does."

"You lost me. Whatever it is, just tell me."

"It would sound . . . crazy."

"Try me."

"Okay, that morning the disaster happened . . . September eleventh?"

Finally, I thought. Finally he's ready to talk about it. "Go on, Cody."

"Okay, Joey and his mom and I got there when the first tower was already burning. We heard that an airplane had hit it. I stood there wishing I had seen it happen."

"So?"

"Just listen." His voice was trembling and he was about to cry. "That's when I started hoping that the *other* tower would get hit by an airplane, so I could see that. Then it actually happened. I saw the other airplane coming, it hit the building, I saw the explosion. I got exactly what I wished for. Who says I didn't make it happen?"

I grabbed him and held him close. "*I* do, Cody. I say you didn't have anything to do with it. Is that what you've been thinking?"

"I can't help it. I know it's weird. It's like it was my fault."

"Cody, it wasn't your fault, okay? Just stop thinking that. When you first got there, it was more like you were watching a video game or a movie or something. It hadn't sunk in yet how real it was. You weren't wishing any of that would *really* happen. The whole thing was caused by the terrorists, not by some idea running through your head. If you had been sitting on the toilet reading a comic book, it would have happened anyway."

The word *toilet* had him smiling weakly. "Didn't Uncle Neal make Liberty stand up by wishing and hoping she would?"

"No, he did it by spending all that time with her."

Cody shook his head. "I can't help it, I still feel like something bad is going to happen."

"To Dad, in Afghanistan?"

"Closer."

"Mount Rainier's going to blow up?"

"Closer."

"Have you been dreaming about being in the mountain lion's pen? You're going to go inside Sasha's pen and accidentally lift your arms above your shoulders?"

With a painful smile, my little brother said, "I've been having bad dreams again. It's weird that you just said that about Sasha. She was in my dream last night. She'd gotten out of her pen and was running all around Seattle. When we caught up to her she was up at the top of the Space Needle, on that ring outside the windows."

"That's not such a bad dream. I kind of like it. She would have been hard to catch, though."

"That wasn't the disaster. It was what happened after that."

"Go ahead, tell me, Cody."

"Uncle Neal was missing. We found him at that place where he used to live, you know, at the beach. Uncle Neal was sick, real sick. I mean, he was . . . dying."

I was so stunned I couldn't think of a word to say. I wondered if I should tell him the truth, right then, but I held back. Instead I said, "Did somebody tell you he was sick? Somebody at the center?"

"Kind of."

"What do you mean, 'kind of'?"

"Kickstand did. He's who told us to go to the beach house to find Uncle Neal. Pretty weird, eh?"

"That's what dreams are for, so you can sort through stuff."

"Can I sleep with you tonight, Shannie? I won't kick you or anything. When Sage let me pet her, I was so happy, but now I feel so sad."

"As long as that grubby blankie doesn't come with."

"I won't need it if I'm with you. Tyler's dad was scary, wasn't he?"

"Yes, but don't worry about it. He isn't thinking about us."

I didn't sleep much that night, and not only because of Cody kicking like he was swimming laps. However he'd done it—maybe it was something like animal intelligence—his little overactive mind had sensed what was happening with Uncle Neal. Every way I looked at it, the time had come. It might as well be me, and it might as well be now.

I waited until after breakfast, then asked my brother if he'd like to take a walk with me down by the creek. When he got to his favorite place, we sat down together and I told him about the cancer. I explained how I'd heard, at the hospital on the Day of the Hawk. I told him all about my talk with Jackie. Cody listened to all of it still as a statue.

"Do Mom and Dad know?" he asked.

I told him they didn't. Cody sat down in the grass and heard me the rest of the way through, up to Uncle Neal being tested again on the twenty-fifth, right after we flew home. I told him that as far as I was concerned, Uncle Neal had already beaten the cancer, he was just waiting to find out. We weren't going to tell him we knew, I said, so Uncle Neal could concentrate on getting well and enjoy the rest of our visit.

I learned a lot about my baby brother that morning, mainly that he was no baby. Cody got it. He completely got it. I wanted to take him in my arms and hug him, but I had a feeling I shouldn't, not right now anyway. I could tell he was mustering up all his bravery, putting all his energy into being strong for Uncle Neal.

We started back. Jackie was expecting us for fresh-baked muffins. On our way Cody said, "Forget what I said yesterday, about something bad happening. Uncle Neal's going to be fine. You know why?"

"Why?"

"Because we would miss him too much."

Later that morning when I was taking out the trash I discovered something familiar in the Dumpster. It was Cody's *Book of Disasters.*

I put down the lid thinking about what this meant. When I looked up I saw Tyler walking up the driveway with a brutal bruise over his cheekbone. "Don't ask," he told me.

"I'm asking," I insisted.

He turned away. "I fell at the shop, okay?"

Tyler was different after that. Stiff. Sullen. We didn't meet at the talking stump any more.

21

HE GOT ME GOOD

It was late in the first week of August. With seventeen days to go I was catching animals hand over fist. I'd picked up a few disposable cameras and was taking pictures of the animals to show my parents. The latest notables were a Canada goose and a river otter. On our way home with the otter, the warning lights on the dash came on. The van trailed a cloud of blue smoke all the way to Cedar Glen.

Tyler was getting off work as we drove in. He'd been avoiding me like the plague. I asked him if he'd take a look under the hood and he said with attitude, "Why doesn't Jackie just buy another one?"

He was just so bristly. I said, "What makes you think she could?"

"Because she's rich."

"I'm not sure it makes any difference," I said back, "but I don't think that's true."

Neal was on his way into the office. "Uncle Neal," I called.

Neal turned back and headed our way. Tyler had been steering clear of him and Liberty, too. "What's up?" Neal said.

"Tyler's wondering about Jackie. If she's rich, that is."

Neal's eyebrows went up. He touched his heart and said, "In some ways, maybe, but not in her wallet. This place is strictly hand-to-mouth, isn't it obvious? She's always on the verge of going under."

Tyler's face was aggressive; his voice was too. "Then how did she get started?"

"With eight baby ducks in her garage, back in north Seattle. People have helped her out along the way because they like what she's doing. You know that the vets are donating their time, same as the volunteers. That's all there is to it. If it weren't for all the people who give ten or twenty dollars a month, there'd be no way."

"Then what about that van? The ambulance? My dad said that's a thirty-thousand-dollar vehicle."

Neal hesitated, then he said, "Well, I can explain that. A few years back, when I had a job and some money in the bank, I donated it myself."

"You're kidding."

Uncle Neal shrugged. "What more can I say?"

Tyler looked at me. "Is that true, Shannon?"

I got a little upset. "I never knew it before, but if Neal said it's true, it's true."

Tyler threw up his hands and walked off. I stood there wishing he'd stayed, said something nice to Uncle Neal and made up. I wished Tyler would go back to working with Liberty and feeling better about himself. But wishing wasn't going to make those things happen.

"Don't give up on him," Neal said.

"He was being such a jerk. And what *about* the ambulance? Can Jackie afford to get a new engine or whatever?"

"It's got a couple hundred thousand miles on it, Shannon, and too many other problems. With as much mileage as the center puts on its ambulance, we need a new vehicle."

"But where will that much money come from?"

"Who knows, but I hope it comes soon. Jackie lives on small miracles. We could use one any time now."

Neal went into the office and I took the otter into the clinic. For ten or fifteen minutes I held various animals while their cages were being cleaned. I felt so uneasy, so apprehensive, and I didn't know why. It's Tyler, I thought, but thinking about Tyler was anything but calming.

I was crossing from the clinic to the house when I heard the screech of tires, a long, heart-stopping screech of tires on the road below the center, then the sudden impact of a vehicle hitting something solid. It wasn't the sound of metal on metal; it was more like a loud *thunk*.

Who or what had been hit? There was no doubt it was bad enough to be deadly. *Cody*, I thought instantly. Where's Cody? I hadn't seen him since we got out of the ambulance and I'd started talking to Tyler. He hadn't gone into the house, he hadn't gone into the clinic. . . .

The creek, I thought. He must have sneaked off to the creek. I could picture it clear as day, Cody hurrying back before I found out, running out of the blackberry vines and right into the road.

I almost fell down, I was so afraid and light-headed. I'd never been so scared in my life. This was the one thing I had to do right this summer, keep my brother safe, and if I'd blown it . . .

"Cody!" I screamed. "Cody! Cody!"

Everybody came pouring out of the center. Everyone but Cody. "Where's Cody?" I screamed. "Where's Cody?"

Fast as I could, I ran down the driveway. Neal and Tyler came running after me. I was infuriated with Tyler, infuriated with myself for losing my focus because of him when he wasn't worth it, didn't deserve it. "I thought you went home," I yelled at him.

"I—I went to the stump," Tyler stammered as the three of us kept running.

On the far shoulder of the road, a woman next to an SUV was kneeling down next to something I couldn't quite see. I thought I was going to be sick. I reeled toward her, covering my eyes.

It turned out to be a deer, thank God. It was dead as dead could be. Thank God it was a deer. The doe had been struck in the head and shoulders. I cast my eyes around looking for Cody and there he was in the open field, running toward us from the creek.

"It's my fault," the lady said. "I was going too fast, and punching up a number on my cell phone. I feel so awful."

Suddenly I recognized the deer, from the fullness of her belly. I said to Neal, who was at my shoulder, "It's the doe that always hangs around the garden. She was probably on her way to the woods down at the creek. Maybe to have her fawn."

"It is her," Uncle Neal said. He reached into his pocket and brought out his pocketknife. "It appears she took the impact with her head, neck, and front legs. The fawn might be alive."

Neal was about to hand the pocketknife to me. It was obvious what he wanted done. With a quick nod of my head I acknowledged I was ready to try it.

Neal sort of nodded back, hesitated, then turned instead to Tyler. "Take this," he said. "Get the fawn out, and do it fast."

Tyler went three shades of pale. "I can't. . . ."

"Come on, Tyler, I can't do it myself with one hand. And I think you can." I'd never seen Uncle Neal this intense.

A moment of confusion, and I realized what was going on. It wasn't because Neal thought I couldn't do what needed to be done. This was about Tyler. It was a test and an opportunity. "Just do it, Tyler!" Neal insisted. "The knife's real sharp. I'll talk you through it. Do it carefully, but do it! Please!"

"Maybe I can," Tyler said. "Maybe I can."

Tyler knelt down, took a deep breath, and opened the pocketknife. He went to work doing exactly what Neal told him. Careful not to cut too deep, he opened up the belly of the doe. Uncle Neal kept giving him careful directions. Tyler laid aside some organs, and then he made a few more incisions—his hands were bloody past his wrists—and then he cut the placental sac free.

"Open the sac," Neal urged. "Hurry, open the sac."

Another careful incision, and the fawn's head appeared. Uncle Neal knelt and wiped the slime off its face, parted its tiny jaws, held its tongue down, and breathed air into its little lungs.

The fawn responded with a kick, a strong kick, and then some more. As it was thrashing around, it opened its eyes.

"Beautiful," Neal said to Tyler. "That was beautiful, Tyler. Cut the cord, or else I'll have to play mama and bite it off. Cut it right here."

Tyler cut the cord, then fell back stunned. Just stunned. Cody and I and the lady who'd struck the doe were all speechless. The fawn was struggling to get to its feet. Jackie was limping down the road with the most amazed expression on her face. By now three cars had stopped and people were crowding around.

"I smell a skunk," somebody said.

I'd been smelling it too, only I hadn't thought about it.

"Guess that's me," Cody said.

People started to back away. "Cody," I said, "you reek. What happened?"

By now the fawn was standing up on wobbly legs next to the body of its mother. "Scoop that fawn up, Tyler," Jackie said. "Bring it up to the medical room. Cody, did you get skunked? How did that happen?"

"I sort of cornered it," he admitted, "down by the creek. I wanted to see what would happen, I guess."

"For heaven's sake, don't go into the house or the clinic with those clothes! Strip outside the back door and head straight for the tub!"

"Yes, ma'am," he said, "but I don't want to miss anything with the fawn."

"Then strip right here!"

"Uh, behind the house sounds like a good idea."

The woman who'd hit the deer followed us up the driveway. Her otherwise immaculate lavender pantsuit had a conspicuous smudge where she'd knelt down. She watched as Tyler set the fawn gently down on the examining table in the medical room inside the clinic. Rosie started drying the fawn with a towel. Somebody was heating goat's milk, and Jackie was talking about what should be added to it. Tyler was standing there watching the miracle of this big-eyed fawn he'd brought into the world. He was in a trance.

I saw him leave the clinic by one of the doors that led out

to the rehab area, and I watched the woman follow him. She was making a call on her cell phone.

My curiosity was aroused. From where I peeked, I could see Tyler had gone to the bench outside Liberty's flying enclosure. To be alone, maybe. No, to be with Liberty. When the woman caught up with him, she started talking to him and Tyler started talking back, not that I could hear what they were saying.

After a minute the woman sat down on the bench next to Tyler, pulled a notepad and a pen out of her purse, and started taking notes.

Back at the clinic, Jackie said the woman who'd hit the deer was the lady who put out the Cedar Glen newspaper once a week. I asked, "What in the world do you think Tyler is saying?"

"No idea," Jackie said. "Your guess is as good as mine. All I know is, right now the center is totally at his mercy. Any piece of bad press could sink us."

I caught up with Cody. He was in the bathtub. Even without his clothes, he was stinking up the place something awful. He looked up at me, smiled, and said, "He got me good."

22

THE CIRCLE OF HEALING

For weeks, Neal had been taking Liberty for walks in the woods. As they'd disappear into the trees I'd see him talking to her. I had a hunch that Neal was telling her about the battle he was fighting and his hopes for the future.

I kept wishing he would talk to me about it. Why not, with our time together running out?

I kept wanting to tell him I knew.

Neal was as aware of the calendar as we were. He started wondering if we wanted to visit this, that, and the other place around Seattle before we left. We didn't particularly care. We liked what we'd been doing. "What about Mount Saint Helens?" he asked Cody as we were rolling south on I-5 one morning. "What's left of it, that is. We could do an overnight."

Cody shrugged him off. "I'm through with disasters," he said.

Neal slapped his hand to his forehead. "I know what. I

can't believe we didn't do this."

With that he swerved suddenly onto an exit ramp marked for Fremont.

"What's this all about?" Cody asked.

"Gotta show you something wild," Neal said mysteriously. Cody bit. "Like what?"

"They got a troll that lives around here. The Fremont troll. Squashes cars like pop cans. Likes to hang out under a bridge, up against the abutments. Reaches up and grabs a car every so often."

Cody was skeptical.

Neal took a couple of sharp turns; a bridge was looming above. "We'll get as close as we can."

We parked and followed Neal toward the abutments. He was sort of crouching and tiptoeing. Suddenly he turned and whispered to Cody, "Got any cuts on you? He can smell blood and he likes kids under a certain size."

"This is like a snipe hunt," Cody said. "There won't be anything there."

But there was. We turned one last corner and were confronted by the upper body of a gigantic troll with a weird silver eye. In one of its hands it was clutching an actual VW Beetle.

Cody crawled under the concrete fingers of the troll's free hand and thrashed around like he'd been caught, screaming bloody murder. I was snapping pictures. Cody ran up the back of the VW and onto the troll's shoulder. "I'm its master!" he shouted.

I got Neal and Cody to pose by the VW in the troll's clutches. Cody was on top of the car flashing the V sign over Neal's head. From here on I'd take lots of pictures, I told myself. The ones of Neal might have to last a lifetime.

Fremont, just north of the ship canal between Puget

Sound and Lake Washington, had lots of other whimsical touches besides the troll—metal sculpture people waiting for a streetcar, for example. They'd been waiting so long they were decorated with balloons and streamers, messages, you name it. There were all sorts of novelty shops, boutiques, bookstores, and coffee shops of course, where you could sit outdoors and soak up the funky ambiance. Neal read the newspaper over a cafe mocha. It was a fruit smoothie for me and hot chocolate for Cody, who sneaked bits from his oatmeal cookie to Sage under the table.

From Fremont Neal took us to the Ballard locks, at the salt-water side of the ship canal, to watch the salmon swim by a plate glass window. The afternoon saw us making the usual round of cold rescues at the vets and half a dozen private homes. Then came a call from Granite Falls, in the foothills of the Cascades. A bobcat, of all things, had been spotted in a parking lot.

"A bobcat is much bigger than a house cat, but not nearly as big as Sasha," Uncle Neal told us. "They mostly hunt rabbits, and they don't come into town. I've never, ever had a bobcat call. We better be real careful. Broad daylight, I dunno . . . there must be something wrong with it."

"Sage will show us where it is," Cody said as we drove into the strip mall where the bobcat had been seen.

"Maybe," Neal said, "but she has no experience with cats."

We drove through the parking lot with no sighting. Neal drove around the back, to the service alley, where there were places for a cat to hide. We got out. I put on a pair of heavy gloves and grabbed the salmon net just in case.

It was a big shopping center, and we split up. Neal, Cody, and Sage went one way, and I went the other.

I poked around the Dumpsters behind the stores. It was broad daylight and I didn't really believe we were going to find anything. Behind a restaurant, with the food smells overripe, I should have been especially on guard but I wasn't. Suddenly an animal, a very large tawny cat, leaped right at me from the rim of the Dumpster. It flew at me so hard I dropped the net and fell flat on my back with my hands up trying to ward it off. Too late. The bobcat's front legs were locked around my neck. I was so frightened I lost control of my bladder, just peed my pants.

A second later I figured out that the darn thing wasn't biting me or scratching me. It was licking my face, like a house cat.

I jumped up and the big cat rubbed back and forth against my leg, purring, like it was overjoyed I had come along.

By this time it was dawning on me that I wasn't in danger. I double-checked myself for injuries. I didn't have any. Fortunately, I was wearing my dark jeans.

I started walking in the direction of the others, calling "Here, kitty, kitty" over my shoulder. The bobcat followed. In case it suddenly turned schizo and attacked, I was keeping the net handy.

By now Neal and Cody and Sage had seen me and were on the way. Sage ran ahead, then put on the brakes just short of the bobcat. The bobcat arched its back like a house cat and hissed. Its teeth and its snarl were impressive. Ears erect, Sage backed off.

Cody's jaw was on the ground. Neal said, "What do you have there, Shannon?"

"I don't get it," I said. "It knocked me down and scared me half to death, then licked my face." I discovered as I spoke that I was still trembling.

"Beautiful coat," Neal said. "Look at all the colors."

Sage was curious, and got a little too close. The bobcat

slashed at her flak jacket with a front paw.

"Wait a second," Neal said. "Look, it's been declawed. Somebody must have raised it as a house pet."

Mystery solved. I was able to talk the bobcat into a carrier without having to handle it or even bribe it with food. It seemed to be used to carriers.

"Sasha had been declawed too," Neal said driving back. "Her owners first saw her as a cute little cougar kitten and thought what a unique pet she would make. Guess what, it didn't take Sasha long to get big, strong, and overpowering. Her claws made short work of their furniture. Guess what, she was acting like a wild animal. The people started to think, next it might be us, an arm or a leg or a face. They had their mountain lion declawed. She kept growing stronger and more powerful but they couldn't let her go. Their cougar couldn't hunt, couldn't protect herself, and she might be dangerous to pets and kids. Sasha was about to be put down when Jackie found out and gave her a home. I'm hoping it might work out the same way for this bobcat."

And that's what happened. Fortunately, Jackie had a spare pen for Bob, as the female bobcat came to be called.

The bobcat was our surprise of the day for Jackie. The new issue of the *Cedar Glen Gazette* was her surprise for us. Tyler's picture, with Liberty on his arm and the fawn at his feet, was on the front page:

MINOR MIRACLE AT JACKIE'S WILD SEATTLE

Tyler Tucker had a life-altering experience last week. He played midwife to a late-season doe struck by this reporter on the rural road in front of the wildlife clinic and rehab center. The doe, unfortunately, was killed outright, but her fawn is alive and the picture of health (above) thanks to a local boy's remarkable grace under pressure. This reporter was eyewitness to the emergency Cesarean section performed with a borrowed pocketknife.

Tyler, son of Gary and Loretta Tucker, told his story as he displayed the bald eagle he is training with the help of one of the volunteers at the clinic.

As he explained, Tyler himself is not one of the volunteers. "I was sentenced to work at Jackie's by the juvenile court judge, as the community service part of my probation. It was the best thing that ever happened to me."

Tucker talked of cleaning the cages of hundreds of small birds and animals alongside the volunteers, and of wearing a bear suit to bring food to a pair of black bear cubs, Gnarly and Sweetness, who are being raised in isolation from humans in preparation for their release next winter in the Cascades. When asked if Sweetness's name was ironic, Tyler smiled and said, "Definitely."

Tucker spoke fondly of a volunteer, a former aeronautical engineer, who introduced him to the bald eagle (above) named Liberty. Nearly fledged, Liberty fell out of a nest in Seattle's Discovery Park earlier this summer. Tyler hopes to be available for taking the eagle to Wild Seattle's school programs around western Washington this coming year.

"Working with wildlife is the coolest thing I've ever done by far," Tyler told the *Gazette*. "If you're messed up, like I was, I definitely recommend it."

A brave admission from a young former offender. "Animals need your help," Tyler said. "They don't care what you look like, what kind of clothes you wear, or if you're popular in school. They only care about what's in your heart."

Asked what he might like to do in the future, when he gets out of high school, Tyler said, "Go in the army or be a wildlife biologist."

Jackie Baker, founder and director of Jackie's Wild Seattle, told this reporter that she believes that people and wildlife are "interconnected, interdependent. Healing them, we heal ourselves. I like to call it the Circle of Healing. Tyler is a perfect example of that circle."

"Unbelievable," I said to Jackie as I finished reading. "This is absolutely awesome."

"Yes," she agreed, "but how will it play at Tyler's house?"

We both knew this could be trouble for Tyler. He must have known that too, when he agreed to talk to the reporter. I had a bad feeling.

23

COYOTE IN A PICKLE

The day after the *Cedar Glen Gazette* came out with Tyler's picture on the front, he ran up the driveway, all winded. It was soon after breakfast, and we were getting in the ambulance. We'd gotten a call about a coyote in downtown Seattle and were on our way.

"Glad you're still here," Tyler panted. "Can you talk for a second?"

"Sure," I said. I got out of the van and we walked off a ways. "I'm history at Jackie's," Tyler said as he gasped for breath. "I just wanted to tell you myself. I had to see you one last time."

"What happened?"

"The article. The things I said in the article."

"Tyler, it was brave, all those things you said. You knew your father wasn't going to like it, but you said it anyway."

"Yeah, he says that's the reason I did it, to get to him. In the back of my mind, I knew he wasn't going to like it. But

I didn't care. For once I wanted to quit being afraid and just say what I felt. Maybe I was even hoping he might understand, when he read it in the paper, might be proud of me. Stupid. Just stupid. I should have known. He says I came off sounding like a hero only because the article didn't tell what I got into trouble for."

"But you *did* tell her about it. Jackie told me. She heard it from the reporter herself. The reporter didn't think it was necessary to go into that."

"Which made it all a lie, according to my father."

"So now you can't work here anymore? Can't finish up your community service the way the judge wanted you to?"

"I guess not. My dad says I can pick up trash along the highway, or serve the rest of the time in juvenile detention, for all he cares. He said I humiliated him. At least my mother liked the article. She said she was proud of me. I couldn't believe it."

"In front of your father, she said that?"

"In front of my father. That was the best part. Hey, don't worry about it, I'm going to survive one way or the other. He can be like that all he wants. I'm not afraid anymore."

"I'll be thinking of you, Tyler."

"Thanks, Shannon. Thanks for believing in me."

"Bye, then," I said, and kissed him on the cheek. "Keep the faith."

"Thanks," he said. "That helps. Where are you guys off to today?"

"A coyote in an elevator in the Federal Building."

"What? In downtown Seattle?"

"They're waiting to see if we can figure something out before Animal Control takes drastic measures."

"What are you going to do?"

"I have no idea!"

"Don't let it take your face off, Shannon. It's such a nice one. Say good-bye to Cody and Neal for me."

With that, Tyler ran down the driveway. We followed him out. He took off up the road—I'd never been that direction—and we turned right, toward Cedar Glen and the interstate.

I had a lot to think about as we rolled south. What was Tyler going through right now? Things could get worse. What was going to happen next, and how was he ever going to find the space to breathe? "Thanks for believing in me," he'd said. Was I ever going to see him again?

When we pulled up to the Federal Building on Second Avenue, it was a madhouse. A crowd was milling around, waiting for a show, and it appeared we were the show. When they spotted the van, all sorts of people started waving. Some ran toward us. We had to double-park. The police, and there were lots of them, said it was okay. There were mobile units from three TV stations in front of the Federal Building, satellite dishes on top of their vans.

Fortunately we'd been briefed on Neal's cell by Seattle police and the security officers from the Federal Building. We more or less knew what had happened. A security guard said that the coyote, being chased by crows, was running back and forth on Second Avenue right during rush hour. When the coyote ran in front of the Federal Building, the automatic doors opened. The animal ran inside.

"Makes sense," Neal said. "It would've been darker in there, looked safer."

"But what was a coyote doing running around downtown Seattle?" I asked.

"Oh, well, they live close by."

"You're kidding."

"Maybe thirty of 'em, down on the waterfront. At night, that's when they're active, cleaning up behind the tourist restaurants. They eat the food scraps some, but mostly they catch the mice and the rats."

"Rats?" the kid in the backseat echoed.

"Great big rats, Cody. Norwegian suckers."

"Norwegian suckers? I don't get it."

"Non-native species. Norway rats."

"I hope we don't ever have to rescue *them*."

"Count me out. City rats are a menace to public health. Which makes our urban coyotes valuable citizens." Neal shook his head, thinking. "Imagine how disoriented and frightened that coyote was when it got caught out after dawn. Which way is my den, where in the heck am I, why won't these crows leave me alone, and where can I find some cover? He runs inside the Federal Building, but there's more people in there, and all he can see that looks safe is to dive inside the elevator. They shut the door on him, then shut down all the elevators in the whole building. It's a big mess, and we're supposed to fix it."

"You mean Shannie is."

"Right. But just if she feels like it."

I didn't know what I felt like. Nervous, I guess. Scared. I wished it was a job for Sage, but it wasn't. Neal thought she would spook the coyote, so we had to leave her in the van. I said, "What's the game plan, Uncle Neal? Net the coyote?"

"Possibly, but I wouldn't recommend that except as a last resort. Once you've netted it, you'll have raised the coyote's fear level through the roof. We need to try to calm it rather than terrify it even more."

"Is that possible?" I was more than a little skeptical.

"Actually, they're gentle creatures, unless they're fighting to defend themselves. I've handled them before."

"You're kidding. You've done this before?"

"A couple of times, but not in an elevator. I hate to see Animal Control tranquilize them. Sometimes they die."

"I don't know," I said nervously. "What exactly would you do if this was your rescue?"

"Go into the elevator, sit down calmly, just start talking with the coyote. Win its trust."

"So you think I can do that?"

"Just if you feel good about it, Shannon. Nothing I've heard has led me to believe this animal is sick. It's just in need of a little help. We'll be right outside. Say Cody's name when you're ready. He'll come in with the carrier, real easy-like."

"What about the net, if we have to net him?"

"I'll have one of the security guards ready with it outside, in case the coyote bolts on us."

"I can't believe I'm going to do this."

"If anybody in the whole world could do it besides Uncle Neal," Cody said dramatically, "it would be you, Shannie."

"Thanks for the vote of confidence, bro."

"Are you going to try, Shannie?"

"They say there's a first time for everything."

In the street, I pulled on the overcoat and a pair of light gloves. Cody grabbed a coyote-sized carrier, I got the salmon net, and the three of us were on our way.

"Give 'em room!" a burly policeman shouted. The crowd fell back and made a corridor for us. The TV cameras were rolling, reporters talking into their microphones, saying stuff about a man and a girl and a boy and a fishing net and Jackie's Wild Seattle. I heard one of them mention our bumper sticker, Turtles for Peace. They were saying lots about the girl because Neal still had the cast on his arm and I was the one with the gloves and the net. The only face in the crowd I really focused on was that of a Native American guy with a dark face and long black hair. He wasn't talking to anybody, just watching very keenly.

The lobby was crowded with people who worked in the Federal Building, policemen and security cops, and the radio and TV reporters. Neal waved for people's attention. Everybody fell silent.

"We'd appreciate your cooperation," Neal said. "TV cameras fine, still cameras bad, unless they're digital, on account of the sound of the shutters. We'll set up a rope line—please stand behind it. When the elevator door is open, please be as quiet as you possibly can. We don't want to startle the animal. My able niece, Shannon Young, is going to attempt to help this coyote out of its pickle. Handling the carrier, that's her brother Cody."

"Where'd the coyote come from?" asked a reporter, holding her microphone toward Neal. The reporter was the supermodel type.

"Just a few blocks away, down at the docks."

"It eats rats," Cody added. "Big Norwegian suckers."

"And what exactly are Norwegian suckers?" the glamorous reporter asked him.

"Norway rats," Cody spoke up. "Non-native species. They're filthy and they're a menace to public health, and that's why the coyotes are good citizens."

The reporters who didn't have recorders or TV cameras were writing all this down. The Indian man was enjoying this.

"Where do you go to school, Cody?" another reporter asked.

"New Jersey. I saw the towers crash down, the World Trade Center towers. My best friend's dad got killed. He was my soccer coach."

"Cody," I whispered, "this might be more than they wanted to know."

"By no means," the reporter said, and another one said, "Are you kidding, this is great." Yet another reporter called, "What else, Cody?"

"Well," my brother said. "Our mother is in Pakistan and our father is in Afghanistan. They help people at the refugee camps. They're with Doctors Without Borders."

"Keep going," the supermodel encouraged him. "The coyote can wait a little longer."

Cody looked at Uncle Neal, who gave him a thumbs-up. "Whatever you feel like saying, Cody. It appears that you're all theirs, and vice versa."

My brother's face lit up. "I know what. My uncle Neal— that's him—he donated the wildlife ambulance that's parked outside to Jackie's Wild Seattle, but it's all broken down. We might not even make it home. Jackie needs a miracle. My uncle can't donate another one to take its place because he's running out of money. He used to work for Boeing. He's an engineer. Maybe somebody else could donate a new ambulance to Jackie."

Everybody in the lobby started clapping.

Suddenly all my tension was gone. The kid had drained it right out of me. Knock me over with a feather, I felt that calm. "Uncle Neal," I said, "I'm ready."

"Let's go to work," Neal said.

Everyone fell silent. The rope line was set up, and the crowd stood behind it. When the time came, the elevator door opened and there was the coyote curled up in the back left corner. It lifted its head and its ears stood straight up. It was looking at me and Cody and Uncle Neal, and past us to a hundred or more very quiet people.

The coyote didn't stand up, just lay there very alertly.

"Looks healthy," Uncle Neal said. "A young one, maybe just a year old. It's a go, Shannon, whenever you're ready."

I hesitated. I pictured the coyote lunging at me like the bear cub and the bobcat. Don't go there, I thought. Don't even think about it.

I took a deep breath. As calmly as possible, I stepped into the elevator.

The coyote stood up. Its ears pointed straight toward me, its tail went straight down.

Behind me, the door closed noisily.

Right away I started talking. I told the coyote how beautiful it was, what beautiful colors it had in its coat, what beautiful eyes, how sorry I was to hear that it was lost.

So far, so good. I decided to sit down. I might look less threatening that way. The coyote locked its eyes on mine as I sat cross-legged across from it. I kept talking. I explained who I was and where I was from, described our house on Liberty Street, described my room, my bedspread and everything on my dresser, then started talking about what a great city Seattle was. "Have you ever been to Fremont and seen the troll?" I asked. The coyote had beautiful amber eyes. They were always right on mine.

By this time I wasn't afraid anymore. I felt calm, even, and I thought how fun this was, what a rush. I thought about Neal. I thought about how much my uncle and I were alike. The coyote truly was a beautiful animal. "Beautiful Amber Eyes," I began to call the coyote, and I meant it. "Beautiful eyelashes, beautiful coat, beautiful wild thing."

The coyote lay back down. There was only about four feet between us.

I had practically hypnotized myself. How long I'd been in there, I had no idea. The coyote's head had been down on its paws for some time now. Its ears were relaxed. I had a feeling it trusted me. It knew I'd come to help it, not hurt it. Animal intelligence.

The time was now. Still talking, I got up on my knees. Still talking, I eased over and sat right next to it, like I might with Sage or Jackie's retrievers. I reached out my hand and touched it on its back. The coyote followed my hand closely with its mouth, but it didn't open its jaws, didn't nip at me. Amazing.

"Beautiful," I said.

I told the coyote how I was going to pick it up, pull it into my body so I could take care of it.

"Let's get you out of your pickle," I said, and then I made my move. I eased my right hand under its chest, slipped under its backside with my left, then pulled the animal into my body. "Cody," I said, not much louder than I'd been talking to the coyote, but loud enough my brother might hear me.

The elevator opened. The coyote's ears went straight up and I felt its body go rigid. In glided Cody with the carrier, the door already open. "He's a friend, he's a friend," I whispered. "He's bringing you a little den to crawl into."

Cody set the carrier down close to me. The coyote looked inside, then glanced at all the faces through the elevator door. Coyote still in my arms, I leaned toward the carrier. It sprang inside.

Cody closed the door. It was over.

24

THANKS FOR THE MICE

My coyote adventure was over, but the day was far from over. Trailing blue smoke, we made about ten or twelve more stops. Late in the day, a policeman pulled us over and wrote Uncle Neal an air pollution ticket. "Seems ironic for an outfit like yours to be getting a citation like this," he said as he gave Uncle Neal a copy.

"That *is* ironic," Cody volunteered from the backseat. I had my doubts whether he knew what he was talking about.

"Wait a minute," the policeman said. "You're the kid I saw on TV at the station during my lunch break. Your parents are with Doctors Without Borders, right?"

"That's right," Cody said, "but pretty soon they're coming home."

"And you're his sister?" the policeman said to me.

"That's my major distinction in life so far."

"I tell you what," the officer said. He took the ticket out of Uncle Neal's hand and tore it in two. "Since your parents are helping out those refugees, I'm going to let your uncle off with a warning, just for being related to you."

"Thanks, officer," Neal said. "We'll park it tonight."

"That's good. We don't want birds dropping dead out of the sky. Still got that coyote?"

Cody leaned forward from the backseat. "We dropped it off with one of the volunteers. She's going to release it down by the docks around midnight."

The policeman gave us a thumbs-up as we drove away. "Cody," I said, "I don't know what we'd do without you."

We were anxious to get home. We started creeping north on I-5, in rush hour traffic. Jackie called to say supper was on the stove. North of the Everett exit, as we were finally making time, we got a call from a man who wouldn't tell me much—he said he'd been trapping, and "Would you take care of the orphans?"

It was from a Cedar Glen address, out past Jackie's on the same road. We were relieved it would hardly slow us down. I spotted the address on a big mailbox in front of an auto shop and a one-story house off to the side. I should have guessed what was going on, but the sign—TUCKER'S AUTO AND TRUCK REPAIR—took me by surprise.

"Uh-oh," I said. "This is Tyler's place, Uncle Neal. That must have been his father on the phone. I think this is one call we should forget about."

I was scared, but Neal didn't look scared. "I've never turned down a call yet," he said calmly. "Let's go see what he's got."

It was well after five and the shop was closed. We walked over to the house. My heart was beating like a sledgehammer. Cody rang the doorbell.

Nothing. Cody rang it again.

Still nothing, then a man's angry voice: "Answer the door, Tyler!"

The door opened, and it was Tyler. He had a fresh bruise, this one along his jaw. He was so embarrassed.

We could see his father on the couch across the room, laughing. "Give it to 'em, Tyler. Let 'em rehab the poor little wild creatures."

Tyler reached for something that must have been placed by the door. He handed me a shoebox. Nested in a clump of dry grass was a litter of squirming baby mice. They were tiny and pink, barely beginning to grow fur. Their eyes were still closed. "I'm sorry," Tyler said. "I'm really sorry."

"They're orphans," his father called. "Parents killed by a trapper!"

"He's been drinking," Tyler said quietly. "This is so ridiculous. I'm sorry."

"Don't be," Neal told him. "No doubt Jackie will take care of them. Your dad's right about that."

"Say good-bye, Tyler," his father warned ominously.

Tyler was about to close the door. He looked desperate.

"What is it?" I said.

Tyler lowered his voice. "Can I come with you guys, right now? I—I think I better."

I looked at Uncle Neal. He looked at Tyler, at his wild hair, the pleading look in his eye, the ugly bruise. "Sure thing," Neal said.

Tyler opened the door wider and stepped out. For the first time I saw his mother. She was watching from the kitchen. She looked like a marble statue that was about to break into a thousand tiny pieces. Tyler turned around and said to her, "Mom, I'm going to spend the night at the center."

"Oh no you're not," his father said, rising from the couch.

"Let's go, Tyler," Neal said softly. "Quick."

"Sorry, Mom. Sorry, Dad, I just think it's best. Kind of a time-out, that's all. Don't worry, it's not a big deal."

We were almost back to the van when we saw Tyler's father in the doorway. With a glance over my shoulder I saw him clenching and unclenching his fists. His face had turned very red.

"Take good care of those mice!" Tyler's dad called.

"We will!" Cody called back. Without a trace of sarcasm, he added, "Thanks for the mice, Mr. Tucker!"

Tyler got in the back with Cody and Sage. He said, "Do you think Jackie will let me stay over tonight? My dad's in real bad shape."

"You know she will," I said. "You can sleep on the couch in the living room. Actually, it pulls out into a bed."

"If I just hadn't started talking to him about the center, about what I was doing there. When I first told him about the bear cub, I thought he'd like it. I thought he'd think it was cool. Big mistake. That's when everything started to get worse. He'd been a little better the last few months, since Social Services talked to him, a little easier on my mom and me. I should have left well enough alone. I wanted him to get excited about what I was doing, about the bear cub especially, about Liberty, too. I should have acted like I hated going to Jackie's, like it was a terrible punishment. That would have made him feel better. This is all my fault."

"You gave your dad a big chance to make a fresh start with you," Neal said. "He's the one who blew it."

"Where will you go tomorrow?" I asked. "What will you do?"

"I sure don't want to go home for a while, not until something changes. Until he gets some help."

Jackie got a few surprises when we drove in—Tyler and
the baby mice. Fortunately there were two evening-shift volunteers in the clinic she could hand the mice off to. Yes
indeed, she wanted them taken care of. She told the volunteers what kind of formula to mix, how much to feed the
mice, to give them a heating pad and make sure it was warm
but not too warm.

Jackie was awfully dismayed to see Tyler's face bruised
again. It was swelling badly. She got him an ice pack while
Neal and I were setting out the spaghetti, salad, and French
bread. I heard them talking about Tyler's probation officer,
about whether calling him might be a good idea. Jackie
thought that the sheriff's department and Social Services
could work together to find emergency foster placement for
Tyler starting the next day. Tyler said he'd think it over
during dinner.

If dinner started out quiet, it didn't stay that way for long.
Jackie got up and turned the TV around where we could see
it. She slipped a tape into the VCR and hit the remote. She
had taped the local news from one of the Seattle stations.

A reporter was talking out in front of the Federal
Building, and there we were driving up, with the camera
zooming in on JACKIE'S WILD SEATTLE and our logos, the
harbor seal and the bald eagle.

Not much spaghetti got eaten during the next few minutes. The tape showed us getting out of the van, Uncle Neal
with his arm in the cast, his *Sage* tattoo, the Mariners cap.
There was Cody taking in all the commotion, and there I
was pulling on the coat and the gloves while the reporter
talked about our unusual mission.

We watched with our mouths open, Tyler too. Next came
the glamorous reporter interviewing Uncle Neal about

where the coyote came from. "Just a few blocks away, down at the docks," he said. And there was Cody, big as life, suddenly entering the frame. "It eats rats. Big Norwegian suckers."

Tyler laughed so hard he was seriously losing it, which was good to see.

"And what exactly are Norwegian suckers?" the reporter asked Cody, kind of afraid of what he might say.

It was all there. "Non-native species," "a menace to public health," and all the rest: how our parents were in Pakistan and Afghanistan, how Jackie needed a new ambulance, all of it.

Jackie hit the pause button. "Best publicity I ever had—even better than the newspaper story. The phone at the office has been ringing off the hook all day. I had to reload the paper in the fax machine. I'm just lucky the home phone is unlisted, or we'd never sleep tonight!"

"Show the rest," I said.

"No, wait." Jackie stepped over to the TV and pointed to a man in the background. "See this man?"

It was the Native American guy with the long black hair. "I remember him," I said.

"Listen to this," Jackie said. "That man left the Federal Building right after you guys did, went to his car, called me up on his cell, and drove straight over here. He ate lunch with the volunteers, ended up spending the entire afternoon here. He left about an hour before you got home. He left this."

Dramatically, Jackie took a slip of paper off the top of the TV and brought it straight to Uncle Neal. She put it in his right hand. It was a check, I could see that. "How much?" I asked.

Neal was so choked up he couldn't even talk. Tyler, sitting next to him, said, "Thirty-five thousand dollars. It's from the Muckleshoots."

"Muckleshoots?" I asked.

"The Muckleshoot Indian Tribe," Jackie answered. "They're from south of Seattle, down near Auburn. It's for a new ambulance. The tribe has a special fund for giving away some of the money they make from their casino. They make gifts to charities and nonprofits. That man you saw at the Federal Building is the one in charge of giving away the money. I guess he liked you guys."

"This is unbelievable," Cody said. "My spaghetti's getting cold and I don't even care."

"There's more on the tape," Jackie said. "We can wait for the rest until after dinner."

"Play the tape!" everybody yelled at once.

Pretty much all that was left was my fifteen seconds of fame, going into the elevator, then coming back out with the coyote in the carrier.

"You have the greatest smile in the world," Tyler said.

I blushed red as the spaghetti sauce. "Yeah, I look great in Uncle Neal's old overcoat. It's a real fashion statement."

25

COMING UP FOR AIR

Of course we had to watch the tape five or six more times. Cody couldn't wait to take a copy home to show to our parents and all his friends in Weehawken. The day he'd do that wasn't far off.

The kid wasn't hyper by nature, but that night it was like he'd knocked over a Starbucks. How he was going to flatten his brain waves and get to sleep, I had no idea. He had me checking the e-mail every time we turned around and kept dragging me into the clinic to look in on the mice. Jackie had said the next few hours were make or break for them. I slowed him down a little by having him feed one of them with the syringe.

Back at the house, Cody enlisted Neal to play soccer Legos on the kitchen table. Tyler and I sat up and watched *Friends* reruns, two in a row. There was so much on Tyler's mind, I figured that watching TV would be a lot easier than talking. At eleven, everything was breaking up. Jackie gave

Tyler a sleeping bag and went into her room, which was our signal to turn off the TV. Cody and Neal headed upstairs.

"Good luck tomorrow," I said to Tyler. "Have you made up your mind what you should do?"

"Yeah, I really think I should call my probation officer, like Jackie was talking about. It's just too tense at home. I might have to stay somewhere for a while, but it should be better in the long run. It's worth a try. If I just go home, my dad might do something stupid. It's a no-win situation if ever there was one. I just wish I could figure a way to help my mom get out of there too."

"Well, I'll see you for breakfast, anyway. Try to get some sleep, Tyler."

"You too, Shannon. Hey, you really did look good on TV."

"No kidding?"

"Seriously."

I went upstairs having no idea I'd see Tyler sooner than breakfast.

I was dead asleep when somebody woke me calling my name. It was Cody, standing by my bed. "Listen," he said.

I was bleary. "What time is it, Cody? Good grief, it's one in the morning."

"I couldn't go to sleep. I'm still too excited. We're going home soon."

"I know, I know. I'm excited too."

"But listen. Tell me what you hear."

Cr-r-ruck! Prruk! Kla-wock! Kla-wock!

"There, did you hear it?"

"A raven?"

"I know. It's Kickstand."

"So? Cody, it's the middle of the night!"

"That's what I mean! Ravens don't talk at night."

"How do you know that?"

"Jackie said so."

I buried my head in my pillow. "Thanks for the information, Cody."

He shook me. "Shannie, Shannie, he's trying to warn me."

"Of what?" I mumbled.

"I don't know, but I have to find out."

"No you don't."

Prruk! Prruk! Tok! Kla-wock!

"There he goes again, and this time he's closer. Shan, he's talking his head off. I have to go see. I just want to go out and see if everything's okay. I'm wide awake anyway."

"You aren't the only one," I said. "And here you've been so good at not being annoying."

"So let's go, Shannie."

"I'm going to walk past Tyler in this nightshirt? I don't think so. . . ."

"Then get dressed and I will too, but hurry. Be real quiet so you don't wake up Uncle Neal."

"You're pushing it," I said, but Cody had already tiptoed down the hall.

A few minutes later we met at the end of the hall. We tiptoed down the stairs. I grabbed the big flashlight in the pantry. Sage was at the front door, waiting.

"Whazzup?" whispered Tyler from the couch as we approached the door. He'd gone to sleep in his clothes. The sleeping bag he'd used for a blanket had fallen off.

"Kickstand is talking," Cody whispered back. "Something's wrong."

"Wait for me. Just gotta pull on my shoes."

The door barely creaked as we let Sage and ourselves out.

It was real dark, with only the sliver of a crescent moon hanging above us. The raven had suddenly fallen silent.

"So, what do you want to do?" I asked Cody. "I just hope this doesn't turn out to be a skunk hunt."

"Let's just see if Sage thinks everything's okay."

Neal's partner was testing the air. Then her ears went forward. She started walking around the back of the office. We followed, quiet as could be.

Sage was waiting at the service gate to the rehab pens, very much on alert. Suddenly she started barking.

Tyler threw open the gate and we ran inside. We could hear someone running, not real close, over toward the deer and the coyote pens, it sounded like. We were stopped in our tracks wondering what it meant, what to do, when the side of the clinic closest to the bears' den lit up with reflected fire.

"Fire!" Tyler yelled at the top of his lungs. "Fire inside the bears' den!"

Without another word, all three of us ran to the back door of the clinic. Inside, I threw on the lights, took three steps, and pulled the fire alarm. Tyler and Cody went straight to the door that led into the bears' den and were back a second later. "Fire in the straw!" Cody yelled.

"I'll get the hose going," Tyler shouted. "You guys get the fire extinguishers!"

We found two extinguishers and raced back to the bears' den. The fire alarm was still going off loud as can be. The noise was almost unbearable, but I was so glad to hear it.

The fire was racing through the straw. At the center of the blaze there was an intense white-hot light. Tyler was on the outside of the chain-link fence putting water on the fire as fast as he could, starting with the source and as far as he could reach. The flames were about to reach the panicked bear cubs in the middle of the three sections. Quick as I could, I pulled on the cord that opened the trap door for the farthest section. The cubs ran through and climbed up the tree, away from the smoke and the heat.

Cody had thrown open the first door, the one from the service path to the inside of the den, and Tyler ran inside hosing down on the fire as fast as he could.

It wasn't going to be enough. Cody and I ran past him, each with a fire extinguisher. We sprayed ahead of us, back and forth, back and forth. And here was Uncle Neal with another fire extinguisher.

As the flames were starting on the wall of the clinic, the four of us mowed that fire down.

Suddenly it was dark. The fire was out. We stood there panting and coughing, the smell of burnt straw and bears strong all around us.

Floodlights came on, and there was Jackie at the clinic door. "Everybody okay?" she cried. "Is everybody okay?"

"Everybody's fine," I said. "Fire's out, Jackie."

"Thank goodness. What happened?"

"We heard somebody running," Cody said.

Tyler was kneeling by the source of the fire. "It's a flare— an emergency flare."

By now we could hear the fire department sirens on the road. "They're quick," Jackie said. "Thank goodness we can send them home."

Sage was sniffing the short red cylinder, partially burned. Cody was about to pick the flare up. "Don't," Neal said. "It might have fingerprints."

"Guess whose," Tyler said bitterly.

"He wouldn't," I said.

"We have flares just like that in our car, in the truck."

"So do lots of other people," Neal said. "Maybe it's not him, Tyler. Let's hope it's not your dad."

The fire department arrived with the police. As it turned out, the sheriff was on his way minutes before Jackie reported the fire. Tyler's mother had called and said that his dad had left the house in a raging temper. She was worried that he was headed for Jackie's to drag Tyler home.

By morning Tyler's dad was in the news. An all-points bulletin had been issued for his arrest. The sheriff had found a piece of material snagged on the top of the chain-link fence in the deer pen. Tyler's mother said it was from his dad's jacket.

By noon Tyler's father walked into a police station in Everett. He turned himself in and admitted he'd done it.

Tyler was back at home with his mother when his dad called from jail. "My mom answered the phone," Tyler said as we sat together later that day on the talking stump. "I was so afraid of how she would handle it. She didn't say much, she just listened. And when he was all done, she just said, 'Tyler and I can't do this anymore. I can't go on being afraid all the time. I'm taking him back to North Carolina.' And that was it. She hung up the phone. So it's settled, we're going, and soon. I guess I won't get to see those two cubs hibernate this winter."

"North Carolina?"

"That's right. Asheville. It's in the Blue Ridge Mountains. My grandparents live there, my mom's folks."

"That's not too, too far from New Jersey," I said. "At least it's on the same side of the country. We could stay in touch."

"You want to?"

"Definitely. We've been through some interesting times together. Interesting times make for interesting people, my dad says. Do you think your mom and dad will ever work this out, ever get back together?"

"I seriously doubt it. She says she's felt so suffocated, she just wants a second chance in life. She said it was hard to stand her ground, though, during that call he made from jail. He begged for her forgiveness, mine too. I'm so proud of her—she stayed strong. Forgiveness, sure, but it'll take time before it means anything. He's always real sorry after he blows up. I only hope he gets it together. I mean, he could've burned down the whole clinic, Shannon."

"And every animal in it."

"I never would've thought he could do something like that. I keep wondering if it's partly my fault, like maybe I pushed him too far, made him flip out."

"Don't even start thinking like that," I told him. "I've watched you all summer. Trying not to be like him. Trying to come up for air. Your mother isn't the only one who was suffocating. You made it, Tyler. Like they say, 'Today is the first day of the rest of your life.'"

26

SO FAR, SO GOOD

It was time for good-byes. Jackie threw a party at the center for all her volunteers, past and present, her friends and neighbors, too. It was a giant picnic that filled up the parking lot and the lawns. Everybody brought card tables and folding chairs and something to eat. There was a live band, kids running around, dogs running around, a raven flying in and out. Kickstand entertained himself barking at the dogs and stealing scraps on one good leg and a stump.

After Jackie cut the cakes, three large carrot cakes she and I had made with garden carrots, she presented us with baseball caps embroidered with big letters in a nice cursive script, *Wild Shannon* and *Wild Cody*. Of course she had one for Neal that said *Wild Neal*. Jackie held up Sage's flak jacket, newly embroidered with *Wild Sage* written across it. Sage appeared from under a table, ready for action, and everybody cheered.

Jackie hugged Cody and me close, then made a little

speech about us, about how she was going to miss us so bad she couldn't stand it, how she thought our parents were the luckiest people in the world, how she'd never had a better summer in her whole life.

There was more. Jackie's eyes went misty as she talked about how much she owed her red-tailed hawk catcher— she bowed to Uncle Neal—and how she wanted to thank everybody for all they'd done "for me and for all creatures great and small these many years."

The next day, the twenty-third of August, it was off to the airport. Jackie said she wanted to say good-bye at the center, so that's what we did. She made us promise to come back, and we told her that would be an easy promise to keep. Cody said, "No more cakes made out of carrots," and Jackie laughed.

We knew, and Jackie knew, that Neal's fateful doctor's appointment was two days later. She said she'd e-mail us as soon as she heard anything, so we should keep checking.

We drove out the driveway of Jackie's Wild Seattle in Neal's old pickup, the three of us and Sage, just like old times.

No stops for hot or cold rescues, just straight to the airport with our new baseball caps on our heads.

Nobody said much along the way. There was too much deep feeling for words. I felt the miles rolling past us and the time ticking down, and I knew this could be our last ride with our Uncle Neal. I fought so hard trying not to cry. Neal was looking straight ahead kind of like down a tunnel. I just hoped he wouldn't look over at me because I was about to lose it. I wondered if Neal was thinking about telling us the secret he'd been keeping, but I was pretty sure he wouldn't, not now.

We were passing the Fremont exit and I thought about Cody running up on top of the troll's head. I turned around with a bittersweet smile on my face and saw the tears running down my brother's cheeks. That did it. My own tears cut loose and a sob escaped me. I looked over at Neal, and he was all startled like the sky was falling.

"Shannon," he said with a catch in his voice, and now I could see his eyes were brimful too. "Shannon, Cody, I'm going to miss you guys something awful."

"Same here," I said, wiping my eyes.

"We're pitiful," Cody said. "All three of us are crying." He turned his face toward Sage and she actually took a lick at him.

After that it wasn't so bad. We started talking about all the things we'd done, all the crazy things that had happened.

When we reached security inside the airport, that's when it got bad again. But this time it was too serious for tears, and I think we were all trying not to spoil it. We mustered up our smiles and laughs and we hugged with "I love you's" that might be last words. "It was hard enough," I said to Neal, "just saying good-bye to Sage at the truck."

"You'll be back," he told me.

"We better be," Cody said, and then he fell apart again, just started bawling.

Uncle Neal looked at him curiously, knelt next to him, and gave him a hug.

"You're the *whole reason*," Cody sniffled.

"The whole reason what?" Neal asked.

"Just the whole reason . . ."

Neal said, "I'll take that as a compliment."

"When are you coming to Weehawken?" I asked.

"How about Christmas?"

"Really?" Cody asked, wiping his tears.

"Tell your mom and dad I'd love to. I've been too long gone. Call me as soon as you get home."

"Promise," we said.

Minutes before touchdown, we spotted Weehawken along the water, across the Hudson River from New York City. We actually spied our house on Liberty Place—half a block from the river on the north side of the street. We saw the shining skyline of lower Manhattan where the twin towers used to stand. I thought of the saying Time heals all wounds.

As we touched down at La Guardia my heart went out to Tyler, wherever he was this minute. The plane came to a stop. Cody and I were holding our breath. We came out of the jetway searching the faces.

Of course our parents weren't there. They couldn't get past security without airplane tickets.

We hustled down the concourse, my brother and I. I asked Cody if he was excited and he said, "Majorly."

We funneled past security into a crowd, where we heard our parents shouting our names. Their voices were the sweetest music I'd heard in my life. There they were, neither one missing so much as a finger. As for holding my breath all summer, I finally let it out.

The day of Neal's doctor visit I spent shopping for school clothes, but I felt like a zombie and came home with only a few things and nothing I really liked. My parents, especially my mother, were still in shock to learn from us that her brother had been sick all this while. They'd told Cody and me not to expect any news until the lab work was done, but

I got up in the middle of dinner and checked for e-mails anyway. There was a new one from Jackie saying that the results would be back either right before or right after the Labor Day weekend. She'd let us know the moment she heard anything.

We didn't hear a thing that Friday. We were going to have to wait for Tuesday, the last day before school started.

Ordinarily we would have gone somewhere Labor Day weekend. This year it was going to be the Berkshires.

We'd canceled those reservations. It didn't feel right. We all wanted to stay close to home.

Tuesday morning found us trying to keep busy. My dad took Cody into the city to indulge his new interest, bumper stickers. They were going to check out novelty shops in Manhattan and maybe even a couple in Brooklyn.

My mom and I started out in Hoboken doing a little browsing. We had herbal tea and some kind of English biscuits at a quaint little shop. "You've done your school shopping and caught up with your friends," my mother said. "I guess everything is over but the waiting. Would you like to go into the city?"

"I thought I would," I said. "But I just can't stop thinking about Neal. I guess I'd rather be home than anywhere else."

"Me too," my mom said.

Back home, I read a chapter from a novel, or rather I ran my eyes over the words. Then I just waited. We got a few phone calls but none from Jackie. Every half hour I would check the computer.

Late that afternoon, word finally came, an e-mail. Surprisingly, it wasn't from Jackie. It was from Uncle Neal himself. We'd never seen him anywhere near the computer. Here's what he wrote:

The most amazing thing happened to me today. In all my years working with animals, I never expected this. Listen up, Cody, this is major. I just got a hug, a big hug, from an eagle. That's right, from Liberty. I can't tell you how much she's been helping me this summer. I'm sorry I didn't tell any of you that I've been sick, but Jackie tells me you figured it out. She said you understand why I didn't tell you. She said my sister would too. I hope she's right.

I can tell you this now. Remember all the times this summer I went walking with Liberty? Taking her with me in the woods? Well, she was talking to me the whole time, telling me I could get through this, that I'd be okay. She'd visit me in my dreams too, flying into my body and wiping out the cancer cells. She gave me so much of her strength. So of course she was the first one I went to today, even before Jackie. I took her out of her pen and headed up into the hills with her. I told her the good news—the tests found no sign of the cancer. It could come back, they warned me, but for now, I'm cancer-free.

When we stopped at the top of the ridge, Liberty turned to me, spread her wings, and wrapped them around both my shoulders. It was the first time I ever knew of an eagle doing anything like that. We stood together on that hilltop a long time, eye to eye. What I figure this means is, she thinks I'm going to be around for a long, long time.

I'll be headed your way for Christmas.

Can't wait.

Love, Neal

"Mom!" I screamed. "Come see. You gotta read this!"

Hyperventilating, I got out of her way. She read it slowly, pausing once to look at me with eyes wide, and then she read it again. I could picture Liberty and Uncle Neal up on that ridge like I was right there with them. My mother jumped up from the computer and we started hugging like crazy. I let out a whoop that might have been heard in Manhattan.

It was definitely heard as far as the front street, where Cody and my dad were getting out of the car.

Cody burst through the front door with a bumper sticker in his hand. "Did you hear, Shannie? Did you hear about Uncle Neal?"

"All clear," I cried. "He's okay!"

Cody gave half a dozen fist pumps, then did a little dance. My father stood beside him, beaming.

"So what's your new bumper sticker say?" I asked my little brother. "Bet you found a good one."

"For Uncle Neal! It's the ultimate of the ultimate!"

Indeed it was. When Neal came at Christmas he brought us a picture of his truck with Cody's sticker slapped on the back bumper:

I INTEND TO LIVE FOREVER. SO FAR, SO GOOD.

AUTHOR'S NOTE

It was a newspaper article that first caught my attention, a profile of a longtime volunteer for a wild-animal rescue and rehab center. Bob Jones had become an urban legend in Seattle. Among other exploits, "Crazy Bob" had rescued a wild coyote from an elevator in the Federal Building downtown, taking it in his arms.

Jones's nickname came from his hair-raising rescue of a fledgling red-tailed hawk from a steep roof during a lightning storm. A baseball cap with his new name was presented to him by Kaye Baxter, founder and director of the Sarvey Wildlife Center near Arlington, Washington, northeast of Seattle. Sarvey, I read, was the largest rehabilitator of raptors in the state, in addition to caring for a staggering array of other wildlife, from baby squirrels to harbor seals.

I had to meet these people and their menagerie.

With his rescue dog Billie at his feet, Bob Jones regaled me with anecdotes of their rescues over the years, while

Kaye filled me in on the workings of the center. Sarvey does wonders for wildlife with the help of countless volunteers. After several visits I came away inspired to write a novel

Some of the rescues in the story are wholly invented, while others are based, sometimes loosely and sometimes closely, on actual Sarvey rescues, most of them Bob's and Billie's. The story line of *Jackie's Wild Seattle* is fictional, as are the characters, though some of them were inspired by real people. Jackie and her "circle of healing" were of course inspired by Kaye Baxter. Uncle Neal was inspired by a combination of Bob Jones and Jeff Guidry, another Sarvey volunteer.

Battling cancer, Jeff devoted himself to and bonded with a bald eagle fledgling named Freedom that had fallen from a nest and would never fly. On the day she was finally to be euthanized, Freedom stood up, signaling her intention to survive. Much later, on the day Jeff was declared cancer-free, Freedom embraced him with both wings.

I am grateful to Bob, Kaye, and Jeff, along with Dorian Tremaine, who shared a day with me in Sarvey's wildlife ambulance, for their enthusiastic support as I researched this novel. I also want to thank my brother-in-law, John Loftus, for introducing me to Sarvey.

The subplot involving the Tucker family's conflict with Jackie's Wild Seattle is entirely fictional. Kaye Baxter has, however, provided opportunities for many troubled teenagers to fulfill their probation requirements through working at Sarvey. Some return as volunteers. Kaye and others from Sarvey, including Freedom and various raptors, have also done numerous presentations in schools all over the Seattle area. A new ambulance was indeed donated to Sarvey by the Muckleshoot Indian Tribe.

For great photos of the wildlife at Sarvey Wildlife Center and much more about Sarvey's mission and operation, I encourage readers to visit their website, www.SarveyWildlife.org.

Another website I hope readers will visit is www.DoctorsWithoutBorders.org. In 1999, Doctors Without Borders was awarded one of the world's highest honors, the Nobel Peace Prize, for their humanitarian efforts around the globe. The organization was active in Pakistan and Afghanistan before and after the events of September 11, 2001.

Durango, Colorado
June 2002

From *Leaving Protection*
Chapter 1

STRANGE, HOW IT ALL BEGAN. Silence hung over breakfast like a spell. Somebody would make an attempt at cheerful conversation and then it would die out like a campfire built with wet wood.

I kept straining for the sound of an airplane motor. My parents and my little sister were doing the same. Maddie, who was ten, was sneaking glances like she might never see me again. My parents were in favor of my plan but they were nervous, too. If everything worked out, I was going to work on a boat fishing the outside waters.

We live in a house that goes up and down with the tides, which are huge in southeast Alaska. We live in the inside waters, in a small cove in Port Protection's back bay. Protection is up in the northern tip of Prince of Wales Island, the biggest of the eleven hundred islands in the panhandle of Alaska, or "Southeast," as we call it.

Port Protection is little, and by little I mean tiny. No streets, no cars, one store. We've got more boats than we do people.

I was born in our floathouse, and so was Maddie. The

moss-covered house and the hodgepodge of cables engineered to let it ride up and down with the tides look like something Dr. Seuss thought up, but my parents get all the credit. One big cedar tree from the mountainside behind us provided all the lumber and the shingle siding. The rusty metal roof is secondhand and so are the single-pane windows, which leak lots of heat. Almost always, there's a fire burning in the stove. Our clothes smell like woodsmoke, but they're clean. We're rich in a lot of ways, but money isn't one of them.

To make some cash money, that's why I was leaving Protection.

"You don't have to go," Maddie said, breaking the silence.

"But I want to," I told her. "I'm so excited I can't stand it. I've been waiting to do this for years."

"We need you on *our* boat," she insisted.

My parents, who knew better, were sitting this one out. "You guys will do fine without me for a few weeks," I said.

"Just because you're sixteen now, and old enough to get a deckhand license—that doesn't mean it's a good idea, Robbie."

I reached over and gave my sister a hug. Just then the whole house pitched up. Books and nicknacks went flying off the shelves, and the sugar bowl sailed across the breakfast table. My father reached out and tried to grab it but missed. When it crashed to the floor, the pieces of china went everywhere.

Quick as can be, a smile replaced my mother's alarm. "Humpback," she announced. We ran outside onto the deck just as the behemoth's broad back gracefully broke the surface only feet away. The whale blew out its pipes as it passed alongside our salmon troller, which was moored at the dock. The spout took its time dissolving into the morning mist.

By now we'd figured out what the whale had been doing under our feet: rubbing off barnacles against the big logs that float the house. It had happened only once before, when Maddie was too young to remember. "It's a good sign for Robbie fishing the big water," my sister cried. My parents nodded like they thought so, too, but it crossed my mind that it could be just the opposite. Not that I'm superstitious exactly, but when you've grown up around the corner from the Gulf of Alaska, you've seen some of what Mother Nature can do.

Right about then we heard the floatplane. A minute later Moose Borden was tipping his wing at us as he zoomed over the back bay. He landed out of sight but was soon motoring up to the house to get me. I'd been ready the day before, but I had to wait until Borden had a paying passenger to drop off at Port Protection. Moose was a family friend, and my flight was going to be free of charge.

Good-byes were brief. "Keep your eye out for a glass fishing float for me," my sister said.

"Definitely," I told her.

"Heads up out there on the ocean," my father cautioned. "Stay focused."

"You better believe I will," I promised.

My mother flashed a confident smile. "Catch a ton of kings, Robbie."

And that was pretty much it. I grabbed my stuff and a couple minutes later I was flying over the floathouse. My family was looking up and waving like there was no tomorrow.